I0600634

No Foreigners Beyond This Point

by Warren Leight

SAMUEL FRENCH

FOUNDED 1830

SAMUELFRENCH.COM

ISBN 978-0-573-69936-8   Printed in U.S.A.   #16131

MUSIC USE NOTE

Licensees are solely responsible for obtaining formal written permission from copyright owners to use copyrighted music in the performance of this play and are strongly cautioned to do so. If no such permission is obtained by the licensee, then the licensee must use only original music that the licensee owns and controls. Licensees are solely responsible and liable for all music clearances and shall indemnify the copyright owners of the play and their licensing agent, Samuel French, Inc., against any costs, expenses, losses and liabilities arising from the use of music by licensees.

IMPORTANT BILLING AND CREDIT REQUIREMENTS

All producers of *NO FOREIGNERS BEYOND THIS POINT must* give credit to the Author of the Play in all programs distributed in connection with performances of the Play, and in all instances in which the title of the Play appears for the purposes of advertising, publicizing or otherwise exploiting the Play and/or a production. The name of the Author *must* appear on a separate line on which no other name appears, immediately following the title and *must* appear in size of type not less than fifty percent of the size of the title type.

NO FOREIGNERS BEYOND THIS POINT premiered at Center Stage in Baltimore, Maryland in their 2002-2003 season. The performance was directed by Tim Vasen and the cast was as follows:

PAULA WHEATON	Carrie Preston
ANDREW BAKER	Ean Sheehy
PRINCIPAL WANG / YING / PEASANT	Ben Wang
TEACHER CHEN / XIAO ER	Jane Wong
VICE PRINCIPAL HUANG / LINCOLN / PEASANT	John Woo Taak
LAO WAN / LAO HU / PEASANT	Les J.N. Mau
MR. WANG / SHERMAN / PEASANT / CUSTOMS OFFICIAL	Andrew Pang
XIAO WAN / XIAO DA	Nancy Wu

NO FOREIGNERS BEYOND THIS POINT was next produced by the Ma-Yi Theater Company in association with Swingline Productions and Culture Project in New York City on September 17, 2005. The performance was directed by Loy Arcenas, featured sets by Loy Arcenas, lights by Japhy Wiedman, and sound by Fabian Obispo. The cast was as follows:

XIAO WAN, XIAO DA	Laura Kai Chen
SHERMAN, WORKER YING	Ron Domingo
TEACHER MING, WIDOW WAN	Wai Ching Ho
VICE PRINCIPAL HUANG	Francis Jue
TEACHER CHEN, PEARL	Karen Tsen Lee
PAULA WHEATON	Abby Royle
ANDREW BAKER	Ean Sheehy
PRINCIPAL WANG	Henry Yuk

NO FOREIGNERS BEYOND THIS POINT was originally commissioned by Baltimore Center Stage's Pealrstone Theatre, where it premiered in November of 2002. It was subsequently produced in New York city by the Ma-Yi Theater Company in September of 2005. Many thanks to both.

CHARACTERS

WIDOW WAN - probably in her 70's. Well fed, long term survivor, few words (all in Cantonese, usually commands), much power.

VICE PRINCIPAL HUANG - late 20's, Northern Chinese, educated, vital but guarded. An outsider in Canton.

TEACHER CHEN - 30's but worn for her years, Cantonese, anxious, kind.

ANDREW BAKER (BAI KE) - 20's, New Yorker, very urban, glib. Wears glasses, no fashion sense.

PAULA WHEATON (WEI TAN) - 20's Waspy New Yorker, striking.

PRINCIPAL WANG - 40's, Cantonese, formal, nervous. The bureaucrat who lives in fear.

TEACHER CHEN - 30's, Cantonese, anxious, kind.

LAO WAN - older long-term survivor; few words, much power.

XIAO WAN - 19, but acts younger; assigned to be the American teachers' maid.

SHERMAN - 20's, smart-ass student; city kid, privileged, General's son (can be doubled by Principal Wang).

LINCOLN - student, late teens/20's, Sherman's sidekick, cynic (doubled by Vice Principal Huang).

XIAO DA - 20's, Northern (Hubei) student, female. Studious, serious: a believer (can be doubled by Xiao Wan.)

PEARL - Straight, initially shy student, female, Cantonese (doubled by Teacher Chen).

TEACHER MING - old lady, long hard life; nominal chair of language department (doubled by Widow Wan, her opposite).

YING - late 30's, peasant; school maintenance man/worker/electrician (doubled by Principal Wang).

CUSTOMS MAN - Young, modern (doubled by Vice Principal Huang).

SETTING

Primarily Da Lang Institute of foreign Trade,
Canton (Guangdong), China

TIME

1980-81

AUTHOR'S NOTES

All rooms are very spartan. Concrete walls, hard, uncushioned furniture, powdery paint.

ACT ONE

(Lights up on the school's official entourage, leaving the American's apartment: **PRINCIPAL WANG**, *[he speaks formally, as if his every word were recorded and could be used against him]. Next,* **VICE PRINCIPAL HUANG** *[the lone Northerner in the group, his manner is different from the others. He's also younger.]. The two men tend to ignore* **MRS. CHEN** *[***TEACHER CHEN***]. She is very nervous, always, and often simultaneously translates for the* **WIDOW WAN** – *Wan is old, imperious, seems to speak little English, and will prove to be the only well-fed person in Da Lang. They wear layers to ward off the cold.* **WIDOW WAN** *bullies* **VICE PRINCIPAL HUANG**.*)*

WIDOW WAN. *(in Cantonese-inflected Mandarin)* Shanghai ren, ni bu xiang diu mian, ni zhou ba ta-men liu xia lai. *(Shanghai man: If you want to save face, you better hope they stay.)*

VICE PRINCIPAL HUANG. Thank you, Widow Wan.

(He nods. She leaves, with **WANG** *in tow.* **HUANG** *turns to* **CHEN**.*)*

VICE PRINCIPAL HUANG. Chen Lao shr, you do think the Americans will renew?

TEACHER CHEN. They did say they've been well taken care of.

VICE PRINCIPAL HUANG. You have a Special Relationship, with Miss Wheaton. I would be very grateful, for any help you can give.

TEACHER CHEN. I will do my utmost.

(She nods, uncomfortably, and exits. **HUANG**, *alone, dictates a report.)*

VICE PRINCIPAL HUANG. Da Lang Institute of Foreign Trade. November 27th, 1980. Memorandum to all departments:

7

VICE PRINCIPAL HUANG. *(cont.)* Widow Wan's generous offer to renew the contracts of Teachers Baker and Wheaton was relayed to the Americans by Principal Wang, and was of course, received with enthusiasm. They did not signal their acceptance right away, but barring unforseen circumstances, they will doubtless continue on as our Foreign Guests for another semester. While there have of course been...growing pains as the administration adjusted to having its first foreigners, much progress has been made since the Americans' arrival five short months ago...on July Four, 1980.

(Under this, **ANDREW BAKER** *and* **PAULA WHEATON** *detrain in Guangzhou [Canton], July 1980. It's hot, and loud. Andrew's gear fits in a duffel bag and back pack.* **PAULA** *has a big trunk, several bags, and back-pack. [He's a little...urban, she's a little Waspy.])*

(A railway announcement, in Mandarin, plays on the station's loudspeakers.)

RAILROAD LOUDSPEAKER. Wang Shanghai de huo che, xian tzai dao di er yue tai shang che.

PAULA. *(very anxious)* You're bringing a typewriter? That's illegal.

ANDREW. Paula, our whole trip is illegal. All the arrangements were made by a Chinatown boss, named..."Kan."

PAULA. He's a friend of my parents. They met him in... Yugoslavia. He helped mother's clinic, dad's school. He –

ANDREW. Right, so...we have no reason to worry. We have no teaching experience. No documentation. No work visas. What could possibly go wrong?

PAULA. *(losing it)* Andrew, this isn't a joke. We have a real chance here to make a difference.

*(They do not notice the approaching entourage [***WANG,** **HUANG, WAN** *and* **CHEN***].)*

PRINCIPAL WANG. Mr. Bai Ke. Miss Wei Tan.

ANDREW & PAULA. Yes?

PRINCIPAL WANG. I am Principal Wang.

PAULA. Yes, of course, Principal Wang! Kan told us about –

(to **ANDREW***)*

It's Principal Wang.

*(***ANDREW*** goes to shake hands,* **WANG** *bows slightly.)*

PRINCIPAL WANG. And this is the Widow Wan.

TEACHER CHEN. She wishes you her welcome after your journey.

VICE PRINCIPAL HUANG. *(shakes* **ANDREW***'s hand)* And I am Vice Principal Huang.

ANDREW. I'm Andrew, this is Paula.

VICE PRINCIPAL HUANG. *(avoiding her offered hand-shake)* This is Teacher Chen.

TEACHER CHEN. Happy Fourth of July.

VICE PRINCIPAL HUANG. Do you have your declaration forms.

ANDREW. Here you go.

VICE PRINCIPAL HUANG. I will handle them.

(He takes them, sees them as a disaster, rips them up, hands them blanks.)

It is more convenient to sign this form, I will fill out the rest for you. Oh, and your passports please.

*(***ANDREW*** goes along with this.* **PAULA** *balks, at first.)*

VICE PRINCIPAL HUANG. Sign here. Very good.

PRINCIPAL WANG. So, did you enjoy your journey?

PAULA. Very much.

TEACHER CHEN. I hope it is not too cold, and not too hot.

PAULA. *(to* **CHEN***)* No, that's right.

VICE PRINCIPAL HUANG. *(to* **PAULA***)* Sign here. Very good. Shall we push on then.

PAULA. Um, I think we still need to clear customs…

ANDREW. And our passports?

VICE PRINCIPAL HUANG. Do not worry. Just this way.

ANDREW. But –

PRINCIPAL WANG. We have a back door.

VICE PRINCIPAL HUANG. *(a bit upset by* WANG*)* So, how was the journey? Did you see the beautiful countryside?

ANDREW. Yes. It was very beautiful.

TEACHER CHEN. You must be very tired.

PAULA. Are you sure we don't need to clear customs. I just –

PRINCIPAL WANG. You have traveled very far. And so, you must be plainly exhausted.

TEACHER CHEN. Everyone at the school is so anxious to meet our foreign experts.

PAULA. We're not really experts…

(She's inadvertently triggered a round of glances and looks. HUANG *takes over.)*

VICE PRINCIPAL HUANG. Yes, technically you are not official Foreign Experts, but you do our school a great honor in bringing your foreign expertise, is what Teacher Chen meant to say.

ANDREW. We can't wait to see the school.

WIDOW WAN. *(in Cantonese)* Mmduck. *(No way.)*

VICE PRINCIPAL HUANG. Duei. *(Got it.)*

(to the Americans)

Of course, but for now you are tired, and need to rest. So you will stay here *(points)* at the Dong Feng Binguan.

(Awkward silence. ANDREW *and* PAULA *are not as impressed as they should be.)*

PRINCIPAL WANG. It is, may I say, the pearl of Guangzhou's hotels. Exclusively for foreign guests. We Chinese, you see, are not even allowed to enter.

PAULA. What? That's not right – that's apartheid.

TEACHER CHEN. It is very expensive.

ANDREW. We're really ok. I mean, I think we would just as soon go straight to the school.

WIDOW WAN. Ju mut ye-ah? *(What is going on?)*

TEACHER CHEN. Kuoi se-arn hoi gan hawk hau. *(He wants to go to the school.)*

WIDOW WAN. Diu. Hou tou yim. Mmduck! *(So fucking annoying. No way.)*

PRINCIPAL WANG. Our school is, I am sorry to say, very backward and we need to complete our special preparations for our foreign experts.

*(**VICE PRINCIPAL HUANG** looks at him.)*

PRINCIPAL WANG. *Guests* – our foreign guests.

VICE PRINCIPAL HUANG. Sometime in the future perhaps, when you have washed and slept and relaxed, and settled in, we will take you out for a banquet.

ANDREW. *(realizes it's a done deal)* Yes that sounds lovely.

(overlapping gooodby)

PRINCIPAL WANG. Until the banquet.

ANDREW. Wonderful.

TEACHER CHEN. We shall call for you at a quarter past six.

VICE PRINCIPAL HUANG. Cheerio

WIDOW WAN. Zoi gin ah.

(They are alone now and exhausted.)

ANDREW. Jesus. I'm ex –

PAULA. Did she say a quarter past six?…We have ten minutes.

*(Before they can exhale, **TEACHER CHEN** returns with what seem to be menus, but are in fact Trade Dialogue Scripts.)*

TEACHER CHEN. Can you read these?

*(They are seated at a small table in front of microphones. **TEACHER CHEN**, wears archaic headphones, cues them. **PAULA** plays A, **ANDREW** reads B. They are a little stiff. **TEACHER CHEN** is very happy.)*

A/PAULA. The Commodity Inspection Bureau is very much surprised at hearing your complaints of this nature. As a state enterprise, we are not allowed to export any

A/PAULA. *(cont.)* faulty goods or blown tins. Furthermore, the goods reached you in June, yet you did not lodge a claim until October. We have every reason to turn down the case, don't you agree?

B/ANDREW. You see. Mr. Chang, *(covers mike, to* **CHEN***)* Should that be Mrs. Chang? Or Miss Chang?

(gets a head shake from **CHEN** *in the booth)*

No? Ok. Just thought – no. Fine.

(continues into mike)

You, see, Mr. Chang, it was a slack season when the goods arrived. To prevent a heavy loss, we had to hold our horse. In September the cases were finally opened with the result that the blown tins were discovered.

A/PAULA. Exactly. That is where the shoe pinches. Even the best canned goods will decay during the hot season in Kuwait. So we've got somewhere at long last.

TEACHER CHEN. Very good. Very good. One more please.

ANDREW. Sorry about stopping for the question, I just thought, since Miss Wheaton is a woman, I should say *Mrs.* Chang –

TEACHER CHEN. We should not change the Foreign Trade dialogues from how they are written. It is more convenient to leave them as is. The students would be confused.

PAULA. Will we get to the school soon, to see the students?

TEACHER CHEN. The school is not yet ready for your arrival. It is more convenient to stay a few more days at the hotel, until everything is ready for your arrival. You are very lucky to stay there, it is the pearl of Guangzhou's hotels.

ANDREW. It's a lovely hotel, and last night, we found a way to keep ourselves busy –

PAULA. *(sotto, embarrassed)* Andrew!

ANDREW. – still it's been almost a week, and Paula, we, are going a little stir crazy there.

TEACHER CHEN. No worries, I have good news. Principal Wang has made arrangements for Vice Principal Huang and I to take you on a tour of the Monument to the 72 Martyrs of the Guangzhou Uprising.

PAULA. That sounds…great.

TEACHER CHEN. And afterward perhaps we can…yum cha.

ANDREW. And we'll get to the school…soon.

TEACHER CHEN. Very soon. *(by rote, but very anxious)* The school is backwards in many ways. Though we have made some progress, we have quite a lot of shortcomings and much leeway to make up before we would expect our foreign guests to stay there. It is much better to stay in the hotel. Now, one more please…

(She hands them more scripts.)

B/ANDREW. FOREIGN TRADE DIALOGUE. LESSON *FOURTEEN*

A/PAULA. A PRELIMINARY INTERVIEW

A/PAULA. Pleased to meet you, Mr. Clark.

B/ANDREW. Glad to know you, *Miss* Chang.

(He has made this change unilaterally.)

A/PAULA. When did you get in?

B/ANDREW. I came on Saturday by the afternoon train.

(As they continue to read their dialogues, he stands and starts to kiss her on the back of the neck.)

A/PAULA. How was the journey? Pleasant, I hope. The weather was not too cold, and not too warm.

(She responds, kissing his hand.)

B/ANDREW. Very pleasant, indeed.

A/PAULA. This is your first visit to the *fertile* lands of Guangdong, I suppose.

(They make their way to their dorm bed.)

B/ANDREW. I've been looking forward to the pleasure of coming in close personal contact with our Chinese friends.

(They climb under the mosquito netting.)

A/PAULA. Mr. Clark, besides doing business you may take this opportunity to see what's really going on in China.

(She starts to unbutton her blouse.)

B/ANDREW. You have certainly achieved great successes. When I get home, I'll be sure to tell my friends and colleagues about this.

(She rides him, while reciting the dialogue.)

A/PAULA. China is a socialist country, and a developing country as well. Though we have made progress, we have quite a lot of shortcomings and much leeway to make up.

B/ANDREW. The Chinese people are known for their modesty.

A/PAULA. There is much for us to learn from you.

(Their pace picks up.)

B/ANDREW. Candid comments –

A/PAULA. – of our friends –

*(**TEACHER CHEN**, students enter, cross stage. **CHEN** speaks into an old microphone.)*

TEACHER CHEN. The Americans are coming.

(The students shout "lai-le" and "Meguo ren shenzai ichee lai-le" as B and A reach the climax of their dialogue.)

B AND A. *(overlapping above)* Always...do...us...good! Oh god yes.

*(**XIAO WAN** appears in their bedroom. She is nineteen, dresses in Hong Kong style acrylic clothing, unlike all the others. She carries a teddy bear.)*

XIAO WAN. Everyone is waiting for you.

PAULA. Oh jesus.

ANDREW. Just a minute Xiao Wan.

*(The lovers go to the hallway, **XIAO WAN** grabs **PAULA**'s hand.)*

XIAO WAN. Make haste. The movie can not start until you sit down.

PAULA. The what?

XIAO WAN. Movie! Movie!

*(They quickly pull themselves together, follow **XIAO WAN** to the basketball court where a projector has been set up.)*

*(**PRINCIPAL WANG**, **TEACHER CHEN**, **TEACHER MING**, students **SHERMAN** and **LINCOLN**, and **XIAO WAN** join in, clapping in unison.)*

PRINCIPAL WANG. These are our very special Foreign guests. Mr. Bai Ke and Miss Wei Tan.

PAULA & ANDREW. *(waving meekly)* Hi.

PRINCIPAL WANG. They will be teaching Spoken English, for this whole semester, or maybe *longer*. To welcome them, we have lodged them at the Dong Feng Bin-guan, for *ten* days. Now they are here. And we give our American guests *four rooms* in the Bachelor Faculty dorm.

(He pauses for this to sink in.)

And their own bathroom. And a servant, Xiao Wan – who is the daughter of our newly recommissioned Nurse Wan.

(She curtsies, very proud.)

And when they need to travel to town, our car and driver. And a refrigerator! –

TEACHER CHEN. *(sotto, to **ANDREW** and **PAULA**)* – although we ask you not to plug it in yet as it is the first one here and we must wait for our chief electrician to read the manual.

ANDREW. Of course.

PRINCIPAL WANG. They are not used to our hardships, and so every thing we can do to make them feel comfort-able, they have only to ask.

(more rhythmic applause)

PRINCIPAL WANG. *(cont.)* It is not as nice as their home, but we give them fresh air and quiet nights and tonight, in honor of their arrival, a movie.

(1970s Chinese movie music swells as the court transforms into a classroom. **STUDENTS LINCOLN** *and* **SHERMAN** *sit first. Then* **PEARL** *and* **XIAO DA** *[PEARL is a sweet, smart, people-pleasing student.* **XIAO DA** *is a strident believer, from the North].)*

*(***PAULA** *enters.)*

PAULA. Good morning class. I see we have –

*(***LINCOLN**, **SHERMAN**, **PEARL**, *and* **XIAO DA**, *seated boy/boy, girl/girl, stand.)*

STUDENTS. Good morning Teacher Wei Tan.

PAULA. Boys *and* girls today. Very good. Sit. Sit. Sherman, and Lincoln, I know, but *(to the girls, who giggle)* your names are…

SHERMAN. Her name is Pearl.

LINCOLN. After the great American writer. *This* one is –

PAULA. She can answer for herself, can't she?

SHERMAN. She is shy so we can help her.

XIAO DA. Xiao Da. Little Big. Because I am first born: Jie Jie, Big Sister, but still little. Xiao Da. From Hubei. In the north.

*(***ANDREW** *arrives.* **STUDENTS** *stand.)*

STUDENTS. Good morning Teacher Bai-ke.

ANDREW. At ease.

STUDENTS. *(repeating, but not sitting)* At. Ease.

PAULA. *(introducing them)* Xiao Da, Pearl.

ANDREW. *(signals students to sit, while sotto voce to* **PAULA***)* Talked to Principal Wang still no textbooks.

(They look at each other, in panic. Quickly debate what to do.)

PAULA. Oh. I know…

(returns attention to class)

Today we're going to try something new. This is free conversation class. We can talk about anything you want to talk about.

(No one says anything.)

ANDREW. Anything at all.

PAULA. So that you can practice your Spoken English.

(No one even looks at them.)

ANDREW. So, who wants to talk about something?

XIAO DA. You have not told us what we should freely talk about.

LINCOLN. Do you have free conversation scripts for us?

PAULA. No, then it wouldn't be free conversation.

(This makes no sense to them.)

PEARL. Should we talk about the damaged cargo and blown tins and how they are not the responsibility of the Commodity Inspec –

PAULA. I think we've already talked about that story enough last week. *(to the boys)* Don't you boys?

*(**LINCOLN** looks at the blackboard, where the phrase:* Good Morning *is written.)*

LINCOLN. *(very stiffly)* Teacher Wei Tan, good morning.

PAULA. Good morning.

(That's it. Followed by more silence.)

ANDREW. OK. Good conversation there.

(more silence)

I know…Why don't we talk about last week's movie?

(No one answers at first.)

PAULA. Oh. Movies. That's always a good conversation topic.

(Still no answer.)

PAULA. Sherman, did you like the movie? Just to make conversation, there is no right or wrong answer.

(They ignore **PAULA**.*)*

ANDREW. You can "pretend" you liked it, or "pretend" you didn't like it…

SHERMAN. Well, I would say –

(right at **XIAO DA***)*

just pretending…

(He checks the room.)

It was terrible.

LINCOLN. Very bad.

PAULA. Really? In what way?

(The boys are now off and running.)

SHERMAN. All Chinese movies have too much propaganda.

LINCOLN. Especially the old ones.

XIAO DA. I prefer the old ones. The new ones have too much romantic.

LINCOLN. Either way you always know what happen. The good PLA soldier reunite the peasant girl with her father who has amnesia from fighting the Japanese…

SHERMAN. *(play-acting now)* Baba? Baba! *(Father?!)*

LINCOLN. *(dramatically over-acting, to* **SHERMAN***)* "Baba?" Wo shr nide baba? Ni shr wode nu'er!

("Father?!" I am your father? You are my daughter!)

(He hugs **SHERMAN**, *whom he has just realized is his long lost daughter. The conversation gets very animated and they act it out, repeating* baba *and* nu'er *through tears of joy.)*

PEARL. Also, you see, the hero never die, even though the KMT or Japanese soldiers are a regiment and he is alone.

XIAO DA. *(upset by the others)* Sometimes he die.

LINCOLN. She right. He die, but it takes a long time for him to die so he can give a speech.

SHERMAN. He has to say, first, long instructions to his fellows about the future and working together, then, he get shot again, and say, "your bullets can stop me, but they can not stop our cause...fight on, Comrades!" Then he die.

XIAO DA. *(passionately)* You forget the most important part, Sherman. Before he die he also should say, "I want to see the Red Flag."

(The boys mock her, in Cantonese.)

PEARL. I like the new ones. The new ones better, much more romantic.

LINCOLN. She right. In new ones, the hero gets his wife back, and his job. He look into her eyes and say –

SHERMAN. "Now that the Gang of Four is smashed, we will be able to modernize the electric plant and produce more and more power for our motherland to advance!"

*(**XIAO DA** is offended by the boys.)*

PAULA. Very good class. All of you speak so well!

*(prompting **ANDREW**)*

Don't they?

ANDREW. Yes. Very well.

XIAO DA. It is now time to talk about how much we like Chinese movies.

(No one says anything.)

PAULA. That's a good idea. I know I've heard some people say movies in China are good because they are educational. Or inspiring.

*(**STUDENTS**, except **XIAO DA**, laugh at this. Especially **SHERMAN**.)*

PAULA. Yes, Sherman.

SHERMAN. If people say it, you mean the teachers, right? Well, the teachers were all xia fang at least once.

PEARL. *(trying to rein him in)* Ttss. Tseh.

ANDREW. Xia fang?

SHERMAN. Xia Fang. Sent down.

XIAO DA. *(correcting him)* Re-educated.

LINCOLN. *(pushing it)* Sent to the countryside to clean shit-houses and shovel night soil.

SHERMAN. Principal Wang, they purge him so many times, he does not trust his shadow.

XIAO DA. Ni gan shenma?! *(What are you doing?)*

> *(**XIAO DA** is shocked by **SHERMAN**'s lack of discretion. **SHERMAN** disdains her as a fun cop. The class spirals out of control.)*

LINCOLN. Bi zhuei.

PEARL. Bei jingde gao. *(Pekingnese poodle)*

SHERMAN. *(at* **XIAO DA***)* Moh cho. *(Shut up/in Cantonese)*

> *(**ANDREW** writes "in any event" on black board to get their attention.)*

ANDREW. "In any event," IN ANY EVENT…

STUDENTS. In any event.

ANDREW. Let's not talk about what the teachers said. What they said is their free conversation, what you say is your free conversation.

LINCOLN. Inside, outside have difference, Mr. Bai Ke. Chinese expression. You see?

ANDREW. *(writes this on the board)* Yes, that's very good. Inside/Outside.

XIAO DA. It MEAN: between two people should stay between two people, within family within family. AND, Sherman, Between Junguo, China and Wai-guo, outside China –

SHERMAN. Outside China, what do you know about –

> *(**PEARL** senses **PRINCIPAL WANG** approaching.)*

PEARL. *(sotto voce)* Haole, haole.

SHERMAN. *(instantly switches gear)* Mr. Bai ke, that is *outside China*, do people like sports?

(ANDREW and PAULA look at each other, not sure what caused the switch.)

ANDREW. Sports. Yeah. I like basketball.

SHERMAN. Can you play center for our team today, Mr. Bai Ke?

ANDREW. Sure.

LINCOLN. Mr. Bai Ke, the school tells us it is your firmest dream to be a writer. Is this true.

ANDREW. Really? The school told you that. Actually, I hope someday to write about China, in fact –

PAULA. Andrew, it's their Free Conversation, not yours.

(As PRINCIPAL WANG moves on. SHERMAN's hand shoots up.)

SHERMAN. Mr. Bai Ke, when the Gang of Four go on trial, will Americans be able to watch it?

(STUDENTS now shout out questions.)

ANDREW. I don't see why not –

LINCOLN. Do all Americans hate the Gang of Four?

PEARL. Do Americans like Lee-gun?

XIAO DA. Lee-gun bu hao. Bad. He want two Chinas. Ca-re-ter much better.

ANDREW. Lee-gun? Reagan. Oh –

PAULA. Reagan? No. No one takes him seriously.

(Questions now overlap into cacophony as PAULA and ANDREW are besieged.)

LINCOLN. What do Americans think will happen in Yugo-slavia, now that Tito die?

SHERMAN. In Poland, they say the ship workers are now rebelling –

PEARL. How come they need Solidarity in a Socialist coun-try?

XIAO DA. They can not rebel. It is a worker state.

LINCOLN. Does every American have a helicopter?

XIAO DA. It's true, in Meiguo, the air is black from pollution?

SHERMAN. That's propaganda.

(to **TEACHERS***)*

They even tell us America lose to Vietnam.

(Nighttime. **PAULA** *does laundry, by hand, in a concrete sink filled with cold water.* **ANDREW** *types, reacts to the campus speakers: Good Night Irene.)*

ANDREW. *(re: music)* That's not just for us, they play it all over campus.

PAULA. Now we know where all those Lawrence Welk albums ended up.

ANDREW. So, I asked Principal Wang about the bicycles today.

PAULA. And?

ANDREW. He said it was "more convenient" to take the car, I said they'd promised bikes as part of our deal. He –

PAULA. They only talk to you.

ANDREW. Who?

PAULA. The Wangs. I can't believe there are nine principals, and they're all named Wang.

ANDREW. No. Actually, only one principal is named Wang.

PAULA. Oh, please. There's the old woman in the silk jacket who doesn't speak English? There's –

ANDREW. No, no. That's the Widow W*an*. *(pronounced Wahn)* She doesn't have a title. She's never here. So I think she's in charge. Like Deng Xiao Ping.

PAULA. Oh.

ANDREW. And *Principal* Wang is the nervous guy who gave the refrigerator speech. He's responsible, but has no power. Then there's *Vice* Principal *Hua*ng.

PAULA. The handsome guy who took our passports? I still think we should get them back –

ANDREW. Don't worry about it. Huang's their fixer, like Roy Cohn. He outranks Principal Wang, I think.

PAULA. Where'd you get that from.

ANDREW. He has a dog. Does anyone else here have a pet.

PAULA. That doesn't make him Roy Cohn.

ANDREW. Also, he's a Northerner. Sherman told me – on the basketball court – Huang doesn't even speak Cantonese.

PAULA. So?

ANDREW. They hate the Northerners down here. They see them as an occupying army that's cut them off from Hong Kong.

PAULA. See this is the problem, everyone talks to you, and I'm just...Paula the invisible Maygoren.

ANDREW. *(correcting her)* Mei-guo Ren. Not –

(off her glare)

I think it's just...how they do business. Teacher Chen yum chas with you. And Xiao Wan loves talking to you.

PAULA. Our maid? Why do we even need a maid? What is that about? God, my hands are cold.

ANDREW. We could send our laundry out. People could use the work.

PAULA. Spoken like a true neo-colonialist. I hate the separate treatment. A car, a maid, a driver, four rooms – They treat us like we're opium traders. I don't want everyone thinking I'm some spoiled rich American.

ANDREW. They don't, they like you. Everyone tells me how lucky I am to have a girlfriend so much prettier than me...

PAULA. They do not.

ANDREW. Ta bi ni shr hen piao liang. She versus you is much prettier... You want to call it a night?

PAULA. There's a huge bag left.

ANDREW. It's like getting out of debt, you can't work your way out all at once.

PAULA. Andrew, there's no debt here. Everyone works together.

ANDREW. "Teacher Wei Tan has skin as pale as the moon, and hair as red as the sunset."

PAULA. Have you seen how the students share everything?

ANDREW. Inspiring.

PAULA. It is. No one has that…pressure. There's no rat race, there's no –

ANDREW. They ate the rats –

PAULA. They don't have car loans, or house loans, they can't fall behind. There's no credit cards, there's no –

ANDREW. No…THINGS TO BUY? No food –

(notices she's shivering)

Are you ok?

PAULA. Raynaud's syndrome. Once they go cold –

(He starts to blow warm air on them.)

ANDREW. Save your hands. We'll do the rest tomorrow, let's get under the mosquito net.

(She smiles, nods, they embrace and she now leads the way to the classroom.)

*(The chairs are in a rough, disordered semi-circle, to facilitate "Free Conversation". **LINCOLN** has just told them the campus gossip: that the Americans are using only one bedroom.)*

CLASS. *(responding to **LINCOLN**'s gossip)* Oooooooooooh.

*(**ANDREW** follows **PAULA** into the classroom, where **LINCOLN** wraps up.)*

LINCOLN. You see, Teacher Wei-tan entered the dining room before the bell was rung.

*(The students laugh. **PEARL** sees the teachers have walked in on them, shushes class.)*

PEARL. Tseh-tseh.

ANDREW. What? What's so funny.

PEARL. *(explaining)* Oh, he is telling a yellow joke about… an unmarried girl who does much romantic.

(ANDREW and PAULA fake getting the joke.)

XIAO DA. *(prosecutorial)* Are you and Teacher Bai Ke married?

(Awkward silence. Giggles.)

SHERMAN. Choose a new topic. Teacher Wei Tan. Go ahead, it is free conversation.

(off of her pause)

There is no right or wrong answer.

PAULA. OK, Sherman: why do you keep that sticker on your sunglasses?

XIAO DA. You are right. The Cantonese are too Western. In Hubei, no one dress this way. But here, it is like Little Hong Kong. Don't care about pitching in, just want to get out. They practice 63 laps in pool because they think that's how long to swim to Hong Kong.

PEARL. Bu shr. *(to the TEACHERS)* Not so.

XIAO DA. Duei duei.

PAULA. I still don't understand, why you wear that sticker?

SHERMAN. Ca-la-wen-kuh-lein-a. Monee talkee, they say in Hong Kong.

(SHERMAN, LINCOLN, and PEARL laugh. PAULA and ANDREW and XIAO DA don't.)

PAULA & ANDREW. What?

SHERMAN. Ca-la-wen Kuh-lein-eh. Yes.

PAULA. *(gets this one)* Ca-la-wen Kuh-lein? Calvin Klein!

LINCOLN. They are Cal-vin Kuh-lein glasses, from Hong Kong.

PAULA. And the sticker?

XIAO DA. Because he want to look like decadent Westerners. With their stickers.

ANDREW. Um…

PAULA. Westerners don't keep the sticker on.

XIAO DA. Oh?

SHERMAN. Ah, but the sticker also tells everyone wo zho ho men.

(Everyone giggles.)

PAULA. Wo-Joe who?

SHERMAN. Zho ho men, run the back door. Many items and privileges can not be obtained in stores, so, I use the back door.

XIAO DA. Nonsense. China does not have a black market.

LINCOLN. *(calmly explaining)* Bu shr. Xiao Da does not know back door. She is from the North. She has many guanxi, so she does not –

PAULA. Guanxi?

PEARL. I think you say connectors.

ANDREW. Connections?

SHERMAN. Her father is Minister of the Guangdong Cereal and Dry Goods Corporation, so she walks in through the front door. Too many ministers from the North.

ANDREW. So, are…most students here children of ministers?

PEARL. *(points at each student)* In finance or trade, or cadres. Or like Sherman, a General's son.

XIAO DA. The children of peasants are also welcome.

LINCOLN. Xia yibeizi.

(Everyone laughs.)

SHERMAN. *(explaining)* Xia yibeizi. Wait until the next life. When you come back…

PAULA. What are cadres? Exactly.

(Everyone looks at her.)

SHERMAN. Surely you are…pulling our leg.

(They can't fathom her confusion.)

XIAO DA. "Cadre" means "the Party representative in your work brigade, or school department, or housing commune."

PEARL. Like the Widow Wan.

(imitates her)

She decides if you can get larger apartment or have a baby or get travel permit to visit relatives if someone die.

*(They see **PAULA** still doesn't get it.)*

SHERMAN. "A penny in the hand of a cadre is worth more than a dollar in the hand of a peasant." Chinese expression.

XIAO DA. In Hubei no one makes such jokes. The school cadres would not allow it.

PEARL. In America, do school cadres say you are now too old to study medicine, even though it is not your fault schools were closed for ten years.

PAULA. It's a little different in the States. We don't really have cadres.

(The students can not comprehend this. Much discussion in Chinese:)

STUDENTS. *(overlapping)* "Shenma?" "Ta shuo "mei yo ganbu." "Zhen da?" "Kai wan xiao" "Tamen bu dong-ah" "Kenan bu shr nega ca-de-re, shr… ca-ra-te?"

("What?," "She says, 'they don't have cadres'.," "Really?," "Really?" "They are joking.," "They don't understand." "Maybe it's not 'ca-de-re', maybe it's 'ca-ra-te'.")

PAULA. English, English. Can we please speak English?

SHERMAN. IN ANY EVENT, we think cadre must be different word in American English.

PAULA. No. Schools just don't have cadres, I'm sure.

ANDREW. They don't. But you still need connections. Guanxi?

SHERMAN. Teacher Bai Ke and Teacher Wei Tan must not have any guanxi if they end up in Da Lang.

LINCOLN. And not even get paid in Foreign Currency.

(Everyone giggles and agrees.)

PAULA. You know what we make?

PEARL. 100 ren men bi a month.

SHERMAN. To be in Siberia of Guangdong Province.

XIAO DA. It is a just salary. The same as all the other teachers.

PAULA. I agree.

ANDREW. And actually, we also will be getting bicycles.

LINCOLN. Xia yibeizi.

(Everyone laughs again. ANDREW *shoots* PAULA *a glance.)*

PEARL. My mother want to know, do you believe in God?

ANDREW. Sorry?

PEARL. Years ago, many fangweilos come here to teach about the baby Jesus.

ANDREW. Fangweilos? What is that – I hear it everywhere.

XIAO DA. *(simply explaining)* Foreign devils…

PEARL. …foreigners.

*(*ANDREW *and* PAULA *look at each other.)*

PEARL. Those fangweilos came to save China. Why did you come.

ANDREW. *(caught off-guard)* "Why did we come?" Um. Well, Paula and I went to High School together, and I'd always had a…crush on her.

STUDENTS. *Oooooh.*

PAULA. Andrew –

ANDREW. So in April, we ran into each other, and she told me she was applying to teach English in China…so I said, I've always wanted to teach in China.

PAULA. Teacher Bai Ke is…joking. We came here, because – well, it starts with our families, really. Andrew's parents are workers, very active in their unions –

ANDREW. Right. Of course. And my mom hates our landlord. She's been on rent strike for like, two years.

PAULA. And my family, they're…professionals, but they've traveled the world over, sharing their expertise, and learning from different cultures. Now, the USA, has always taken the Capitalist Road.

(off students' excitement)

And I know, I know you think there are some good… things about that, but there are also many bad ones. We don't have free health care, or barefoot doctors, or free education for all. And I wanted to see for myself what it was like to live in, and learn from, a country that has taken…the Socialist Road.

(She finishes, somewhat proud of her speech; so is **XIAO DA***, who claps.)*

XIAO DA. Capitalism is "a dying man who is sinking fast."

SHERMAN. *(stands, looks East, ala Mao)* Only Socialism can save China!

(The others start to laugh. Uncontrollably. **LINCOLN** *recovers.)*

LINCOLN. He is joking, of course. The truth is, China is very backward. Very poor. Everywhere in world, Chinese people are very rich, except in China. Always so. China never change.

XIAO DA. Bu shr. Already many things change. School get Toyota van, Hitachi TV…foreigners.

PEARL. And also, because of you they move the sign back.

PAULA. What?

LINCOLN. *(off of their confusion)* The sign on the road.

PAULA. What sign?

PEARL. This is why they keep you in the hotel for ten days. You could not come here until they move it. Before it say: "No Foreigners Beyond This Point."

LINCOLN. It still does, they just move it back three miles.

*(***LINCOLN*** *does not notice an approaching shadow.* **PEARL** *signals* **SHERMAN***, who interrupts* **LINCOLN***.)*

SHERMAN. *(shifting gears fast)* Mr. Bai Ke – "pair sunglasses" or "pair *of* sunglasses"?

*(Suddenly the students straighten out all their chairs, and sit up straight. **PAULA** and **ANDREW** can't figure out why the mood has shifted. A moment later, **TEACHER MING** walks in and students immediately stand. **MING** is an old woman seen the night the Americans were introduced to the campus. She's no older than **WIDOW WAN**, but she has had a much tougher life, and it shows.)*

PAULA. Hello?

TEACHER MING. I am –

CLASS. Good morning Teacher Ming.

TEACHER MING. *(in an older style of English)* Chairman of Language Studies.

PAULA. Can I help you…

TEACHER MING. Am sorry to be late. Please accept my humblest apologies.

ANDREW. Yes of course, Teacher Ming. We met the night of the movie. You are welcome to…

TEACHER MING. Please forgive me, my English is very poor. I speak Russian, and Yugoslavian. And Esperanto, of course. Eduku, traduku, lernu.

*(**TEACHER BAI KE** and **WEI TAN** look at her blankly.)*

TEACHER MING. But my English, you see, is very poor. So I come as your humble student.

ANDREW. We're teaching Free Conversation today.

TEACHER MING. Yes. I know. Please…go on.

*(**MING** takes a seat, front and center. As the students sit, they push their chairs neatly back in rows)*

ANDREW. We were talking about the sign on the –

XIAO PEARL. *(stopping him)* Teacher Bai Ke, you said it needs the article "of," is that for plural only, pairs *of* sunglasses, or also when it is just one pair sunglass?

ANDREW. *(realizes the fun is over)* Oh, uh, I see.

("teacher mode")

This is a little tricky, Pearl

(points to her)

has one *pair of glasses.* Xiao Da also wears a *pair of glasses,* and so together we have two pairs of glasses.

PAULA. I don't think that's completely right. Two *pair* of –

(ANDREW and PAULA have a private "discussion" about spoken versus British English.)

PEARL. But why if there is only one, is it a pair?

SHERMAN. *(pouring it on now)* And why is one pair called glasses, not glass?

PAULA. Well –

XIAO DA. English, may I say, is not very logical.

PEARL. Not like Chinese.

TEACHER MING. *(first addresses teachers from her chair, then stands)* Just so. In Chinese, our language is five thousand years old, and so, everything is quite evolved, and therefore logical. No grammar. Just say what word should logically come next, and that is Chinese. No need to bother with plurals or tenses.

(now facing students)

For example, you all know the poem, by Li Bai, from the Tang Dynasty.

(She writes five characters on board.)

Chuang. Qian. Ming. Yue. Guang.

Bed. Front. Bright. Moon. Light. No verb, no article, but we read these characters and immediately see an image: "The moon is shining over my bed." Foreign languages are immature, or…less efficient. Their letters hold no meaning and lack logic. So they must use grammar. But if you study hard, English can be learned, and knowledge is always worthy of pursuit. There's another poem….

(STUDENTS drift away, MING writes more characters as PAULA watches, takes photos of Ming and characters. As

ANDREW *leaves,* SHERMAN *buddies up to him.* XIAO DA *takes all this in.)*

(Cross-stage, HUANG *emerges, summons* MING.*)*

TEACHER MING. *(nervous)* Jin tiande ying wen ke. *(Today's English class)*

The Free Conversation class was very lively. Teacher Bai Ke and Teacher Wei Tan try to explain grammar but English is so illogical, even they became confused.

VICE PRINCIPAL HUANG. They are poorly trained. I'm afraid we will have to make do with them, until we receive certification for bonafide Foreign Experts.

TEACHER MING. What they lack in experience, they make up for in enthusiasm.

VICE PRINCIPAL HUANG. Do you think then, they are here to indoctrinate?

TEACHER MING. The Americans? No, not at all, Vice Principal Huang. They are very...open, and bright-eyed. I will of course keep my eyes open for signs of Western decadence and corruption. Xie-xie.

(XIAO DA *now passes* TEACHER MING *in a corridor on her way to see Huang.)*

XIAO DA. Jin tiande meiguo lao shrde ying wen ke.

(Today's American teacher English class)

The Americans teach class in an unstructured way and even make us move the chairs out of order. Much time is wasted in pretend discussions. Student Sherman in particular talks too much nonsense. When Teacher Ming arrives, it is of course much better.

VICE PRINCIPAL HUANG. This Sherman –

XIAO DA. He is the ring leader.

VICE PRINCIPAL HUANG. Tell me his Chinese name, Xiao Da. I will see to it he admits the error of his ways.

XIAO DA. Of course, he is Yeh Ping...

VICE PRINCIPAL HUANG. General Yeh's son? I see. Well, thank you, Xiao Da.

(The American's bare living room. **PAULA** *fiddles with the lenses of her camera. Radio plays jazz.* **ANDREW** *arrives, hand-weighing a letter for* **PAULA**.*)*

ANDREW. Mail call. Another group letter, from your mom. And unless she has 30 year-old scotch tape like they do here, I'd say you're not the first person to read her letter.

(She eagerly opens, reads it.)

PAULA. Don't be paranoid.

ANDREW. And still no textbooks. Stuck at customs. How do they expect us to teach with no textbooks. Today's class...a trainwreck.

*(***PAULA*** nods while he speaks, but has mostly been reading her letter. Radio switches to announcer from music.)*

VOA ANNOUNCER. That was Willis Conover's House of Jazz. And now, the news, from Voice of America in Special English.

ANDREW. Oh god not more Special English.

VOA ANNOUNCER. President. Jimmy Carter. said today. that.

ANDREW. Speak faster! Faster!

VOA ANNOUNCER. The. American hostages. in Iran. should not.

ANDREW. – shouldnotbecomeapartisan political issue in the –

VOA ANNOUNCER. become. a partisan, political iss-

ANDREW. We've heard this.

VOA ANNOUNCER. -sue. in the Presi –

ANDREW. Twice today.

VOA ANNOUNCER. – dential, campaign. against –

PAULA. God.

VOA ANNOUNCER. – Ronald Reagan, former Governor Of Cali –

*(***ANDREW*** turns it off.)*

PAULA. My parents might leave the country –

ANDREW. If Reagan wins?

PAULA. It's not just Reagan. She's talking about how they have an empty nest now. Number one son, Karl, is in Zimbabwe, helping to set up their mental health system. Emma's in El Salvador, working with the mothers of the disappeared.

(reads this aloud)

"And Paula is teaching business students at her Junior College in China."

(realizes, once again)

They think I'm a failure.

*(**ANDREW** has been half-listening, while keeping an eye Huang's office.)*

ANDREW. They do not.

PAULA. Chaos, the family dog, gets two more paragraphs than I do. I'm an afterthought.

ANDREW. Paula, I'm sure they like you as much as the dog.

PAULA. Also, I think they're going through a trial "separation."

ANDREW. You're kidding. Why?

PAULA. She doesn't talk about it, Andrew. It's just, her letter doesn't say a word about how they're doing, or their plans. They're socialists but they're still WASPs – No news is bad news.

ANDREW. I'm sorry.

(He consoles her, and spies on window.)

PAULA. You'd think I'd do better here, I've been trained since birth to read between the lines.

ANDREW. God, no one says anything, ever? Really? That sounds great. My family – loud. Very loud.

(squinting out window)

Uh oh.

PAULA. What?

ANDREW. I just saw Teacher Chen pass Xiao Da. Didn't Chen tell you she was going into the city for her day off.

PAULA. We yum cha-ed a few hours ago, she was about to leave.

ANDREW. And now she's there. At Vice Principal *Hua*ng's.

PAULA. You're being paranoid.

ANDREW. Bu shr. I think they have to give reports on us.

PAULA. What could she possibly tell him?

*(Cross-stage, **HUANG** debriefs **TEACHER CHEN**.)*

TEACHER CHEN. Jin tian: there were shoe prints on the toilet seat in their apartment. I asked Teacher Wei tan if any workers came by, and she said a worker, Ying I think, had been by to fix an electrical device. I think Worker Ying wanted to use a toilet, he is from the country and has never seen one. I think he did not know the seat is to *sit* on.

VICE PRINCIPAL HUANG. Thank you Teacher Chen. I hope this did not interfere with your day off.

TEACHER CHEN. No bother. Xie-xie.

*(**TEACHER CHEN** leaves Huang's office. **HUANG** immediately goes to see **WAN** and **WANG**.)*

WIDOW WAN. *(to the men, in Mandarin)* How could this happen?)

VICE PRINCIPAL HUANG. It will not happen again, I assure you.

*(**HUANG** nods to **WANG**.)*

PRINCIPAL WANG. *(reads announcement)* Announcement to all workers and teachers entering the American's apartment. Please do not use their toilet as it is a privilege only for the foreign experts to use.

*(A tinny recording of Edelweiss comes over the loudspeakers. Under the mosquito netting, **ANDREW** and **PAULA** sit up. All around them in the dorm, the sound of men clearing their throats. And spitting – a morning ritual.)*

ANDREW. Edelweiss? They're playing Edelweiss at six am, on a Sunday morning. I travel nine thousand miles –

(more spitting sounds)

PAULA. It drowns out the spitting. Why does everyone spit so much?

(Now, loud sounds of a mob chasing something. In Cantonese:)

BACHELOR TEACHERS. Koi hai bindo ah? (*Where is he?*)
Hai li to! Hai li to! (*Over there!*)
Da se gaoh! Da se gaoh! (*Get the dog. Get the dog!*)
N'hoi bai koi zaoh! (*Don't let him get away!*)

(A dog barking. The sound of clubs being swung. The dog whelps.)

PAULA. What's going on out –

ANDREW. *(he goes to the window)* Oh god. Don't. Just stay there Paula.

PAULA. Why? What is it?

ANDREW. Vice Principal Huang's dog, they're…chasing it.

*(The dog whelps now. It makes a horrible series of sounds. **PAULA** and **ANDREW** wince at every howl. At last the dog stops howling. Laughs echo.)*

PAULA. Oh god.

*(**PAULA** covers herself with the comforter. **XIAO WAN** appears.)*

XIAO WAN. Good morning. Are you ready for pork fried noodles?

PAULA. I don't feel much like eating right now.

XIAO WAN. Are you all right? Shall I get my mother? She is a real nurse – educated before Cultural Revolution.

ANDREW. Miss Wei Tan's fine. She's just –

XIAO WAN. If she feel sick, make sure she see a doctor who went to school more than 17 years ago. 17 better than 7.

ANDREW. Miss Wei Tan's fine. She's – she has a dog at home.

XIAO WAN. Vice Principal Huang is not from Canton.

ANDREW. I don't understand.

XIAO WAN. Well, he is from the north, and so he thought everyone feeds his dog because they like it; but the Cantonese, they feed the dog so he get big enough to eat. Everyone is laughing at Huang.

ANDREW. Oh.

XIAO WAN. He sent from the North, to watch you, but he does not even know *us*.

ANDREW. He's *what*?

XIAO WAN. A Northerner, he think he can boss us around and make us kowtow. But today, the worm turns.

ANDREW. No, the other part. He was sent to –

XIAO WAN. Today we will eat meat for the first time this month. Big feast, I will make sure you are invited.

PAULA. We don't…beat dogs in America. They are pets.

XIAO WAN. If you beat the dog, it tastes much better than if you slit its throat. So they use sticks.

ANDREW. Oh.

XIAO WAN. The Cantonese, they say, eat everything with four legs except a table. And everything with wings except a plane. This is a joke.

ANDREW. Yes.

XIAO WAN. Not all animals taste better if you beat them. I think not a cow. Is it same for American cows, Teacher Wei –

ANDREW. *(exiting to wash)* Teacher Wei Tan doesn't eat meat.

XIAO WAN. Neither do we. The only way we get meat at the school is if a water buffalo dies of old age in the fields. Even then, all we get is the chewy fat. This joke is because all the meat goes to Guangzhou, to the cadres.

PAULA. I'm sorry. I don't find these jokes funny, Xiao Wan.

*(A awkward silence. **XIAO WAN** starts to curtsy and leave as **WORKER YING** enters, carrying an antiquated spray can.)*

YING. *(to* **XIAO WAN**, *in thick Cantonese)* Ho'm hoah?

XIAO WAN. *(to* **YING***)* Ho'ah.

> *(to* **PAULA***)*

> I forget. Worker Ying must spray your room. Do not worry, he will not use your toilet again.

> *(***YING** *starts spraying. But can not take his eyes off* **PAULA***.)*

PAULA. I don't know if we want him to –

XIAO WAN. Everyone wants DDT, it's very good. But because you are Foreign Guests, you get the most.

> *(***PAULA** *reacts badly to "DDT.")*

PAULA. *(shouting)* Andrew!

> *(to* **YING***)*

> It really is not necessary to spray that. Bu hao. Bu yao.

YING. Ha lo. Ha lo!

PAULA. Listen to me! Comrade. We don't want DDT. No Stop! Stop!

YING. Ha lo. Ha lo!

> *(***ANDREW** *re-enters.)*

PAULA. Andrew, it's DDT.

ANDREW. Ying, Ying. M'goi Ying, gole. M'o-yaoh. Go'lah. M'goi sai le. *(Ying, Ying. Thank you Ying, enough. We don't want it. Enough. Thank you so much.)*

> *(***YING** *looks at* **ANDREW***, stops.* **XIAO WAN** *and* **PAULA** *look at* **ANDREW** *too.)*

YING. Sik gong ah. Sik gong ah? *(You understand/speak?)*

ANDREW. Yut dee dee. Zoi gin ah. M'goi sai le *(A little. See you. Thank you.)*

> *(***YING** *laughs and smiles and backs out.)*

YING. Sik gong ah. *(He understands.)*

XIAO WAN. Teacher Wei Tan, you have not eaten your pork fried – ?

*(***PAULA*** signals no.* **XIAO WAN** *leaves.)*

PAULA. Cantonese? You speak Cantonese now! When did –

ANDREW. All the students – that's what they speak, on the basketball court. Kai-dai. Yo mama. It's no big…

*(***ANDREW*** watches* **XIAO WAN** *go to* **VICE PRINCIPAL HUANG***'s office.)*

XIAO WAN. Jin tian, guan yu meiguo laoshrde bao gao *(Today's report on the American teachers)*: The Americans are still sleeping in one bed. They have been here four weeks and use one and one-half bars of jasmine soap and two and one-half rolls of toilet paper.

VICE PRINCIPAL HUANG. Have they asked you questions, or made any comments about our school.

XIAO WAN. Miss Wei Tan was very upset about how your dog…ran away, Vice Principal Huang. She told me to bring you this, I think it is a letter.

(Concerned, he takes it.)

Also Mr. Bai Ke told Worker Ying not to spray DDT, in Cantonese. Xie-xie.

PRINCIPAL WANG. *(speaks into microphone)* Reminder: As our institute becomes truly international, students and faculty must take special care to speak in only the People's Tongue of Mandarin. Cantonese is prohibited at all times on campus.

VICE PRINCIPAL HUANG. *(reading* **PAULA***'s letter)* Dear Vice Principal Huang, I am so sorry about what happened to your dog. I have a dog at home in New Jersey. Her name is Chaos, because that is what she causes. All the time. Your dog was very sweet, and well behaved. I know keeping pets, and kindness to dumb dogs, must seem here to be another spoiled Western luxury, but I thought you might want to know that Teacher Bai Ke and I were concerned for her, and you. Sincerely, Teacher Wei Tan.

*(***VICE PRINCIPAL HUANG*** places the letter in his wallet. Cross-stage,* **ANDREW** *and* **PAULA** *in their apartment,*

with **TEACHER CHEN**, *and* **PRINCIPAL WANG**. **CHEN** *and* **WANG** *are uncomfortable, and hiding their embarrassment, as they look at a table with sodas and candies.*)

TEACHER CHEN. It can not be helped.

ANDREW. Really? The whole class just forgot they have an exam to study for, so none of them can come to our party?

TEACHER CHEN. We are very sorry to be the bearers of bad news.

ANDREW. Usually they are so organized.

PAULA. We understand. Maybe after the exam.

PRINCIPAL WANG. Yes, perhaps some time soon the festivity can be rescheduled for a more convenient time.

ANDREW. Well, we have some extra candy and soda. Would you two like to stay.

PRINCIPAL WANG. Us. Stay? We cannot, you see. We must help the work brigade with the Mosquito Abatement Program.

TEACHER CHEN. Yes. And we know how busy you are with your writing, Mr. Bai Ke.

PAULA. Oh, well. Some other time.

TEACHER CHEN. Yes, very good. Zai jian.

(**WANG** *and* **CHEN** *leave.* **ANDREW** *and* **PAULA** *stare at each other.*)

ANDREW. I told you they'd cancel. Principal Wang, I expect it from, but Teacher Chen –

PAULA. Cut her a break. She's trying. She went through a lot. I think maybe her husband left her –

ANDREW. What the hell happened here? It's like dawn of the dead out there, everybody walks around all day long, with their books in their hands, memorizing this week's party directive because God forbid anyone dares to say what they really think or feel. Everything's by rote. You know that the students aren't taught phonetics, they've learned to spell every word in English by memorizing the order of the letters.

PAULA. It's how they learn Andrew. For 5000 years. I'm sure you have a better system, but –

ANDREW. Have you noticed that everybody here is a little – I don't think we got the whole – Principal Wang can not look at us when he speaks, Teacher Chen shakes like a leaf, Xiao Wan is fourteen going on three. This whole place is like a giant outpatient clinic.

PAULA. God you're negative – and she's nineteen.

ANDREW. What?

PAULA. She's nineteen. Teacher Chen told me. And that teddy bear she clutches, was given to her by her dad whom she hasn't seen in twelve years –

ANDREW. Jesus.

PAULA. And her brother may be a little, damaged or –

(PAULA now looks up and sees XIAO WAN, who has been watching them.)

PAULA. Xiao Wan!

XIAO WAN. Good evening. May I replace your thermoses?

PAULA. Xiao Wan – do you think you can knock or ring the bell.

XIAO WAN. I have a key so there is no reason to bother you.

ANDREW. Still, it's something we –

XIAO WAN. My daddy writes from Hong Kong how happy he is to hear I work for you. He send many special gifts in next package. He wants to be sure you teach me much Spoken English. He says someday it will help me to get out –

ANDREW. Xiao Wan, can I ask you a question? To practice English. When you left here this morning…you went to see one of the Principals. Huang, maybe?

XIAO WAN. He is not a principal.

ANDREW. Whatever, the point is –

XIAO WAN. You are thinking of Principal *W*ang. *Hu*ang just arrive when you do. He is Vice Principal in charge of the Da Lang Foreign Expert Language Program.

XIAO WAN. *(cont.)* Although he says we must remember you are not official foreign experts, and have no training really, but because you are here maybe someday we will get them.

PAULA. Oh.

ANDREW. But you did go see him?

(She nods "no.")

ANDREW. Xiao Wan, I saw you there.

XIAO WAN. *(upset)* I am sorry Mr. Bai Ke. Miss Wei Tan. After I go to see you, I must go to see him, it is my job. If I don't tell him about you, they take my job away, and my –

PAULA. It's ok. Xiao Wan.

XIAO WAN. No. I don't want to tell them things about you, but they tell me it is my duty. To tell them when you go to town. Or who come to see you.

*(***XIAO WAN*** clings to ***PAULA*** like a child.)*

ANDREW. Who tells you to – ?

*(***PAULA*** shoots him a glance – leave her be. She calms ***XIAO WAN.***)*

PAULA. Who tells you?

XIAO WAN. The cadres, my mommy say so also. Because they decide if Daddy can ever see us. Or if my brother can get treatment. He is not right in the head. He saw Daddy marched around in dunce cap and get beaten. Very badly. Then after they arrest Daddy, they took Mommy away. Xia fang. Because she was a nurse who used Western medicine. For three years my brother and I not know if they are alive or dead. We are like poison. No one go near us or look at us. No one talk to us, except to shout. No home. Nothing to wear, or eat. Just walking, all day long. He go wrong in head. Now sit in chair and rock. Just like so. All day long. Please don't tell them you saw me.

*(She cries and cries, like a baby. ***PAULA*** rocks her gently.)*

PAULA. It's ok, honey. It's ok.

XIAO WAN. Please don't tell. Please don't tell. Please…

*(***PAULA*** *holds* **XIAO WAN***. Sound cue: Red Guard denunciations, in Chinese, blending into a mass rally of Mao announcing the Cultural Revolution.)*

End Act One

ACT TWO

*(**PRINCIPAL WANG** and **TEACHER CHEN** sit in front of **ANDREW** and **PAULA**'s TV, in folding chairs. **CHEN** is angry with **WANG**, and tries to get him to shut up.)*

TEACHER CHEN. They're not interested in the old stories. Bu yao zai shuo. Bu yao zai shuo. *(Mind your speech.)*

PRINCIPAL WANG. Stinking number nine they call us. Lowest of the low.

ANDREW. I'm sorry, I don't follow.

TEACHER CHEN. He is talking nonsense.

PRINCIPAL WANG. Ten years of nonsense. During the turmoil, they rank the enemies of the revolution.

TEACHER CHEN. Gole. Gole.

PRINCIPAL WANG. Teachers and intellectuals were ranked lowest.

TEACHER CHEN. *(overlapping)* Ni shuo shenma. Haole. Hao le Gole.

PRINCIPAL WANG. *(plowing through)* Beneath landlords, and old capitalists, and common criminals. Then, stinking number nine –

TEACHER CHEN. *(sternly)* But things are much better. China is very backward, but it is now on the right track.

PRINCIPAL WANG. Too late. The best years of my life, all the teachers lives, were wasted. Now we are used up.

TEACHER CHEN. Moh cho-ah! *(Shut up!)*

PAULA. Um…more tea?

WANG & CHEN. No. Bu keci bu keci bu bu –

ANDREW. It's no trouble.

*(As **ANDREW** gets up, **WANG** corrals him.)*

WANG. And the students? All they learned was slogans. They know nothing. Nothing. Nothing.

TEACHER CHEN. Teacher Wei Tan, I will help you.

*(**PAULA***, who wasn't going to get up, now goes off to kitchen with* **TEACHER CHEN.***)*

PRINCIPAL WANG. The Da Lang Institute we are in now was attacked by Red Guards. They invade and make teachers walk around in dunce cap; kneel on crushed glass. The police do not protect us. More Red Guards come, and we barricade ourselves in the school. They take over the camera factory. And shoot at the school. Night after night. In the morning they are gone, but the next night they come back, and fire only in the dark. They are cowards you see.

For a week we live like this, then Teacher Liang, Teacher Chen's husband, a very capable math teacher, he borrows a cannon, from sympathetic other guards and, calculating exactly, shot the headquarters of the bad guys on the first shot –

ANDREW. The camera factory? Across the road?

PRINCIPAL WANG. Just so. After that, Liang was sent very far away. Xia fang. Many teachers here sent away. And those who could not read became the teachers. Some still here. Teacher Chen was sent away for reading music. Bourgeois Western music they call it. Teacher Ming and I spent three days, and three nights burning every English book. Every dictionary she and I owned. Page by page. Professor Liang, he committed suicide.

*(**TEACHER CHEN** and **PAULA** enter.)*

ANDREW. I'm sorry.

TEACHER CHEN. Shush. He justs talks about the past. Now things are better. The Gang of Four will go on trial for what they did to the country. And we will soon watch it on TV.

*(**PRINCIPAL WANG** reacts to something.)*

PRINCIPAL WANG. Who is there?

(All get tense. **XIAO WAN** *enters. They relax.)*

XIAO WAN. Xiao Wan. It has not started yet?

TEACHER CHEN. Mei yo. *(not yet)*

XIAO WAN. I want to see Jian Qing fried in oil, alive.

PRINCIPAL WANG. She should be sliced up, into pieces.

TEACHER CHEN. No, she should be made to suffer for the rest of her life. Kept on the edge of starvation and frostbite and exhaustion like we were. Give her just enough food so she won't die.

*(***ANDREW** *and* **PAULA** *look at* **TEACHER CHEN**. *They have not seen this side of her.)*

PAULA. Who wants tea?

EVERYONE. Bu keci. No thank you. Bu-bu-bu.

*(***PAULA** *fills their cups, they tap their fingers thank you.* **WANG** *again reacts before the others.)*

PRINCIPAL WANG. Who is there?

(Turn to see **TEACHER MING**.*)*

TEACHER MING. Just Teacher Ming. Please excuse my interruption. I overhear your television, and even though my English is very poor, I thought perhaps you need a translator. I see you are in fine hands. Very sorry.

*(***ANDREW** *gets up, gives* **MING** *his chair.)*

ANDREW. Please come in.

XIAO WAN. Look. They start. There he is. Chen Boda!

TEACHER CHEN. And Wu Faxian!

PRINCIPAL WANG, TEACHER MING. Shame. Shame.

(They hiss at the screen. Like fans at a wrestling match.)

PAULA. He looks…drugged.

PRINCIPAL WANG. They say he gets injections, to keep him alert until the trial end.

ANDREW. I think you mean, alive.

PAULA. *(covering this)* Are those people…the jury?

TEACHER CHEN. We don't have juries. They are all judges.

XIAO WAN. Look, there's Wang Hongwen.

(boos)

TEACHER MING. *(explaining)* The one they call the helicopter.

PRINCIPAL WANG. Because you see, he rise, straight up, to power. But now, look at him.

TEACHER CHEN. Look at his hair, like a common criminal.

XIAO WAN. *(enraged)* There is Jiang Qing!!

TEACHER CHEN. Mao's widow. The dragon whore.

PRINCIPAL WANG. Huai dan.

TEACHER MING. Zhao gong! Zhao gong! (*Confess. Confess.*)

XIAO WAN. I hope she kill herself.

PRINCIPAL WANG. She is too ugly to die.

TEACHER CHEN. She get power, ruin China. Look! She has no shame.

(All boo her. Losing control.)

PRINCIPAL WANG. She is still arrogant. You see. The others are beaten. But she still treats everyone like filth.

(They vent ten years of humiliation and fury. It escalates to a shocking level of anger.)

ALL. Sa ta! Sa ta! Ta ma de! Diyuni! Magahayah! Sa ta!

TEACHER CHEN. Murderer! Murderer! Confess! Confess!

(Boo. Hiss. "Kill her." Then suddenly the screen goes blank.)

XIAO WAN. Oh no. What happen to the picture.

*(**ANDREW** checks the TV as **WANG**, **MING**, **CHEN** stand, panicked.)*

ANDREW. Could that be all they show?

XIAO WAN. *(at the window)* It is off in the student hall too.

PRINCIPAL WANG. They show more tomorrow.

PAULA. You don't have to go.

CHEN. I'm so sorry.

ALL. Xie xie. Zia jien.

(They close the door.)

ANDREW. What the hell was that about?

PAULA. How did they even…Did you invite them or –

ANDREW. Xiao Wan let me know it was on and –

PAULA. Because they really – I'm honored they watched with us. I mean, they really, the barriers really dropped. They finally let us in.

ANDREW. Ah-huh.

PAULA. Andrew, something really changed. They lost it… in front of us.

ANDREW. Yeah they did.

PAULA. *What?*

ANDREW. It's just…OK: Everyone's now officially allowed to vent. It's the new line. The Gang of Four – those ten geriatrics – they're the scapegoats for the whole Cultural Revolution. The teachers have to go to work tomorrow with people who tortured them, but now those people are off the hook. It's all wrapped up. Case closed. It's not just a show trial, the entire country is a show jury.

PAULA. Did you even see what just happened here?

ANDREW. Yeah. I did…The barriers really dropped. OK.

PAULA. *(walking out)* Not all of them.

(Morning. **ANDREW** *and* **PAULA** *in* **PRINCIPAL WANG** *'s office.)*

PAULA. We hope we're not disturbing anything.

(Note: **PRINCIPAL WANG** *answers* **ANDREW**, *even if* **PAULA** *asks the question.)*

PRINCIPAL WANG. I trust everything is satisfactory for you.

PAULA. We want to thank you for coming over –

PRINCIPAL WANG. I have good news. Electrician Chou tells me soon he will give the go ahead for you to start up the refrigerator.

PAULA. That's great. The school is doing so much for us. Even so, we keep wondering, and we know how hard the school is trying on this – is there any word yet on –

ANDREW. When do our bicycles arrive?

(*PAULA shoots him a "what are you doing" glance.* **VICE PRINCIPAL HUANG** *and the* **WIDOW WAN** *"happen" to walk by.*)

VICE PRINCIPAL HUANG. Zao.

WIDOW WAN. Mo mut yeah? (*Anything going on?*)

PRINCIPAL WANG. Mo-ah. (*Nothing.*)

(*Their presence felt, they walk on.*)

PRINCIPAL WANG. Ah yes. The bicycles, you see, are a difficult item to procure. They are rationed and so unfortunately we must wait for the proper time. It cannot be helped.

ANDREW. AH-HUH. Any idea when that will be?

PRINCIPAL WANG. I will send another cable to the Department of Foreign Trade Education, and the Department of Transportation this afternoon.

PAULA. The problem is...We promised this Foreign Expert from the Guan Li Institute –

PRINCIPAL WANG. Oh, Miss McCafferty?

ANDREW. You know her, of course.

PRINCIPAL WANG. Yes, everyone is happy that the Scottish Old Maid has returned. She is a..."Special Friend of China."

PAULA. Anyway, she wrote and told us to meet her in Foshan on Sunday. She even offered to provide us with educational materials for our school.

PRINCIPAL WANG. This weekend? I don't know if we will be able to arrange for the car and driver on the day off.

PAULA. Oh no, that's ok. Miss McCafferty gave us instructions on which bus to take. Although, of course, if our bikes come before then –

PRINCIPAL WANG. Bus? *Bus?* You are our guests. Please. It would be more convenient if we arranged the trip.

ANDREW. I really don't see how that could be more –

PRINCIPAL WANG. I will immediately cable the Ministry of Travel Documentation, and ask them to issue papers which will make the trip much more convenient.

ANDREW. The thing is, Miss McCafferty goes often without permission –

PRINCIPAL WANG. That can not be so.

ANDREW. Oh.

PRINCIPAL WANG. We just have to inform the department for reasons of safety. There may be rascals in the countryside who out of ignorance would harm foreign visitors. And of course there is no reason to take the bus.

ANDREW. We take buses all the time in New York.

PRINCIPAL WANG. In any event, you will find it much more convenient to wait until the car is available. Don't you agree?

ANDREW. No, actually. I don't agree.

PAULA. Andrew.

PRINCIPAL WANG. What?

ANDREW. Look Principal Wang, wouldn't it be easier to be straight with us. You never meant to give us bikes, we're never going to get them. This whole cabling thing, is just a charade. Is that about right?

(**ANDREW** *just walks out.*)

PAULA. I'm so sorry, Principal Wang.

PRINCIPAL WANG. I should send those cables post haste.

PAULA. Yes, of course.

(starts to leave, stops)

Last night, we were so glad you and Teacher Chen came over. We felt less isolated…And we'd like to be able to have more nights with our campus friends. For some reason, the students do not come visit us, even when we ask them to. One student said this was a school policy. Can that be true?

PRINCIPAL WANG. A policy? Of course not. I do not know why someone would say such nonsense.

(seizing an opening)

Tell me who told you that, and I will be sure to set the record straight.

PAULA. Maybe we're the ones who misunderstood.

PRINCIPAL WANG. Our students, because of the turmoil, lost many years of education. Some are very lazy. These students often use the wrong words.

PAULA. I think that is what happened.

PRINCIPAL WANG. Then this was in a beginner class, I take it?

PAULA. Oh gosh, I don't honestly remember.

PRINCIPAL WANG. When the name comes to you…Can you tell me? Thank you so much.

(He returns to his paperwork, she holds for a beat, leaves. PRINCIPAL WANG exhales. VICE PRINCIPAL HUANG walks by, PRINCIPAL WANG jumps. They separate. TEACHER CHEN enters. In two separate corners, CHEN debriefs, and WANG makes and announcement. HUANG moves between them both, criticizing WANG.)

PRINCIPAL WANG. This is to remind all students and teachers that to avoid misunderstanding –

TEACHER CHEN. Teachers Wei Tan and Bai Ke were disappointed when the school was unable to obtain travel documentation for their trip to Foshan –

VICE PRINCIPAL HUANG. Principal Wang admits the error of his ways in telling the Foreign Guests that some students are lazy –

PRINCIPAL WANG. – no one other than school administration shall inform our Foreign Guests of policies concerning their tenure here.

VICE PRINCIPAL HUANG. – and that in the countryside there are peasants who might engage in rascal behavior.

TEACHER CHEN. I told them sometime in the future the school will arrange for an overnight stay in Foshan. This good news greatly improved their moods.

(The Americans' bedroom. **ANDREW** *types,* **PAULA***'s in her own world, with a letter from home. They wear several layers of clothes.)*

ANDREW. *(reads his entry)* Sometimes I think Wang wants to help us. Then – he sits there and just lies to our face. But it's not lying. It's being a good host. To not give bad news. And you're supposed to be a good guest, and just accept that yes means no. And no means, what? Not yes – you never get to yes. There's not even a word for "yes" in Chinese. Or for "no."

PAULA. It's very good, Andrew.

ANDREW. I can't figure anything out here. One minute I think it's communism that's crippled it, then I think, no, this is still Confucianism, then –

PAULA. Could you maybe give it a rest, for one night?

ANDREW. Teacher Bai Ke sincerely apologizes for once again lapsing into negativism.

(sees she's upset)

Paula, I'm sorry.

PAULA. It's not you. Well, you're not helping, but – I got another one of Mother's group letters to the family today. I told you something was up. They're selling the house. All my things are there.

ANDREW. Reagan might not win.

PAULA. No, they're getting divorced.

ANDREW. I'm sorry.

(consoles her)

PAULA. They're selling the house, I don't even have a place to live.

ANDREW. What do you mean, of course you do.

PAULA. Andrew, we've been together 24 hours a day, seven days a week, from the moment we got here.

ANDREW. It's just flown by, hasn't it.

(off her)

Paula, once we get out of here, we'll be fine.

PAULA. Not at your place, it's a tiny studio.

ANDREW. I could get shelves. We could look for a place. Although do you have any idea what rents are –

PAULA. I've always been Dr. Wheaton's daughter, or Karl's kid sister. Now I go half way around the world, and the few times I'm even by myself, all anyone asks is "where's Mr. Bai ke?"

ANDREW. Paula –

PAULA. Which is exactly why I didn't want to be in a relationship in the first place.

ANDREW. Paula – it's a little late for that. Unless you're just sort of slumming with me til we get home.

PAULA. No, Andrew. Please, I just – I've never had my own place. Do you understand?

ANDREW. Yeah. I get it.

(An awkward silence. He starts to pace as she exits. Transition to just before dawn. Instead of the usual crickets, today there is the sound of ducks, quacking, and then Edelweiss blasts over the loudspeakers. Followed by spitting. Followed immediately by **XIAO WAN** *'s entrance into their apartment. She curtsies.)*

XIAO WAN. Good morning Teacher Bai Ke. I hope the ducks did not prevent you from sleeping like a log.

*(**ANDREW** goes to the window.)*

ANDREW. There must be fifty thousand ducks out there. Where did they come from?

XIAO WAN. Hunan.

ANDREW. Oh. Hunan ducks. Of course. And why are they here.

XIAO WAN. They are marching to the border.

ANDREW. Oh.

XIAO WAN. The long march. *(giggles, proud of her pun)*

ANDREW. Those people with sticks? They're not from the Da Lang commune.

XIAO WAN. Oh those. Maybe they are *also* from Hunan. It *might* be that some of them are looking also for extra duck eggs to take to the free market in Guangzhou.

PAULA. *(returns from shower, shivering)* God that was cold. Xiao Wan, how do you stand the cold shower.

XIAO WAN. I use the communal hot shower that is behind the kitchen.

PAULA. There's a hot shower?

XIAO WAN. Teacher Chen already ask if you can use it. And the Widow Wan tell that before you can use they would need to shut it down. To fix. And that would take two or three months. Teacher Chen say, you of course would reject this proposal, because you do not like special privilege.

ANDREW. That's…just…perfect.

PAULA. *(opens breakfast bowl, takes a bite)* This is good, what is it?

XIAO WAN. Rice with candied pork fat.

*(**PAULA** discreetly spits it out.)*

XIAO WAN. You are lucky to get so much fat, everyone else gets only grease today.

PAULA. Do you think we could get, oh I don't know…duck eggs?

ANDREW. Xiao Wan says they sell most of the eggs on the black market –

XIAO WAN. Free market. China does not have black market.

PAULA. Oh well.

ANDREW. How much?

XIAO WAN. They will get in trouble if they sell to you, you are our Foreign Guest.

ANDREW. How much? Please, my pants are falling off of me. Teacher Wei Tan and I are losing too much weight.

PAULA. I am not.

ANDREW. How much for a duck egg?

XIAO WAN. Seven fen I think.

ANDREW. Here's two kwai. One for them, one for you. See if you can get a dozen

XIAO WAN. *(very eager)* I will wait til xiu-xi, *(mimes nap time)* then I send my brother. Because he is bad in the head, no one will watch him. Also, if you want many eggs, or a whole duck, American dollar is better. They can use to buy rationed goods from Friendship store, and sell for much more again. In Hunan.

ANDREW. I thought they couldn't get into those stores?

XIAO WAN. All Chinese citizen forbidden from entering them. But maybe they know a Visiting Overseas Chinese who goes in and buys, *a bicycle* – which otherwise needs ration coupon.

ANDREW. And that person sells this bike for cash on the free market. Where?

XIAO WAN. Behind the train station is the best one. Although no Chinese or foreigners or even overseas Chinese are allowed to go to that one because it is of course outlawed. But it is the best –

PAULA. Andrew, you are not going over there.

ANDREW. What are you my mother, now?

PAULA. *(fast, so* **XIAO WAN** *won't understand)* Canwe notdothisinfrontofthe –

ANDREW. Xiao Wan, could you go file your report on us.

XIAO WAN. *(takes the hint)* No bother. Oh, I forgot to tell you, Teacher Chen say to tell you she will come over soon. Zai jian.

(She leaves.)

PAULA. Andrew. What are you doing.

ANDREW. I just want a bike, so that when I'm about to lose it, I can peddle into the paddies until –

PAULA. You're flirting with her, bribing her to buy you things on the black market –

ANDREW. Flirting. Are you nuts? Now who's the one who's paranoid. I'm not –

TEACHER CHEN. *(arriving)* Mr. Bai Ke, Miss Wei Tan. I hope I am not interrupting.

ANDREW. No, I was just leaving. And Paula was hoping you two could yumcha. Weren't you, Paula.

(He goes. **CHEN** *sees* **PAULA** *is upset.)*

PAULA. Come in, Teacher Chen.

TEACHER CHEN. Is this an inconvenient time?

PAULA. No. Please. Come in.

TEACHER CHEN. I am sorry the overnight trip to Foshan was cancelled. Sometimes, a "cold wind from the north" blows. You see.

PAULA. Yes. I understand.

(A silence. **CHEN** *senses* **PAULA** *is upset.)*

PAULA. Would you like some tea.

TEACHER CHEN. Bu-bu-bu-bu-bu.

PAULA. *(pouring tea)* Andrew was um…in a rush. To get to the post office.

TEACHER CHEN. Yes. I saw. He is very devoted to you.

PAULA. I'm glad.

TEACHER CHEN. Teacher Ming tells me you bring much life to your class.

*(***PAULA*** *doesn't respond.)*

TEACHER CHEN. I have found much hope, in teaching. Great joy. I think you find this too.

PAULA. Yes. Thank you.

TEACHER CHEN. Oh also, I meant to tell you. Tonight we celebrate the Harvest Moon. A festivity. Teacher Ming is having a very special banquet.

PAULA. Oh…I hope you have a nice time.

TEACHER CHEN. You too. She want me to invite you and Mr. Bai ke to her house tonight. A quarter past six. The party will start, and you will happen to walk by the family dorm, Room 103, and hear it. She will then be obliged to invite you in so as not to offend our Foreign Guests.

PAULA. Thank you Teacher Chen.

TEACHER CHEN. Big banquet. And harvest moon cake. I will see you tonight. Zai jian.

(Time shift.)

ANDREW. Paula! Paula!

*(**ANDREW**, on a heavy three speed, bikes cross stage, as peasants gawk.)*

PEASANTS. *(in Cantonese)* Loila loila! Gweilo loila! Lo fan. Ha-lo.

(Look, look. Foreigner, look. Hello!)

*(The peasants wave, **ANDREW** signals them to be quiet. **ANDREW** dismounts. He wants to be a hero, but no one is there to see his arrival.)*

ANDREW. Paula! Paula!

*(**SHERMAN** sneaks up on him.)*

SHERMAN. MR. BAI KE!

ANDREW. Sherman.

SHERMAN. So, the rumor is true. You were able to purchase a Flying Pigeon and Golden Phoenix –

ANDREW. I have no idea what you're talking about.

SHERMAN. Your bicycles. The school is now quite in a quandary, but they can not say anything because they promise you bikes all along.

ANDREW. They won't take them away?

SHERMAN. Oh come on you know they can not. Because to take them would be to admit you have them. But, since they did not give them to you, the only way you could have obtained them, is via the black market. But since China does not have a black market, you can not possibly have them.

ANDREW. And the whole school knows this.

SHERMAN. Every villager from here to Guangzhou saw it with their own eyes – you have struck a blow for equality.

ANDREW. Let's not go –

SHERMAN. Even though the Phoenix is a peasant's bicycle, everyone is quite happy for you.

ANDREW. It's a peasant's bike?

SHERMAN. It is the one they use when they transport a couch or bed home.

ANDREW. Huh.

SHERMAN. Next time you go to the Black Market, or better…the Friendship Store, do your homework. Study hard.

(*sotto*)

I can help.

ANDREW. Pardon?

(*sees* **SHERMAN** *is serious*)

The bikes were a one-time thing.

SHERMAN. They don't have to be. We should have Sino-American friendship.

(*off* **ANDREW**'*s reaction*)

You can get into the foreign currency stores, but you have no currency. My fellows and I have currency, but can not get into the stores. Now, if we work together, put both oars in the water, you see –

ANDREW. You want me to smuggle for you.

SHERMAN. Not smuggle. Goods already here. Together we buy them, then my fellows and I sell. Mai/mai. Buy sell. Yes.

ANDREW. No, I'm not a mai/mai ren.

SHERMAN. This is why you need my help. You do not have to answer now, think it over. OK…

(**SHERMAN**, *arm around* **ANDREW**, *walks him off.*)

(*In Room 103,* **TEACHER MING** *and* **XIAO WAN** *and* **TEACHER CHEN** *and* **WORKER YING** *bring out huge trays of food. Their radio plays…Edelweiss. The small table is ridiculously stacked with dishes. Food is placed on their plates from all sides.* **PAULA** *poses everyone for a group photo.* **ANDREW** *comes in, late.*)

PAULA. Everybody, lai le lai le *(come, come)*. Yi-er-san. *(one-two-three)*

EVERYBODY. Che zi. Che zi. *(The equivalent of "cheese." Actually means "eggplant.")*

TEACHER CHEN. Fish – two kinds sauce. Ginger and sweet and sour.

TEACHER MING. *(proud)* Boiled chicken.

XIAO WAN. *(explaining)* Chicken is very luxury. Cost much more than duck, pork or even beef, which is really water buffalo.

TEACHER CHEN. Moss sour.

YING. Gai lan ah.

TEACHER MING. *(to* **ANDREW***)* Here is a very special drink just for you. Mr. Bai Ke.

(She hands him a cloudy drink [the others have orange soda]. **ANDREW** *is about to sip it.)*

TEACHER CHEN. No wait. Ming, Ming. You must make a toast to the harvest.

*(***MING*** *nods. Everyone lifts a glass of orange soda.* **ANDREW** *holds his special, cloudy drink.* **MING** *takes it all in:)*

TEACHER MING. I never imagine I see day like this.

(almost overwhelmed)

When I was young, we have nothing. Nothing to eat. My father kill by the Kuong Ming Tung – you know, Chaing Kai Shek's men? I was eight year old. I eat maybe…every three days as a girl. I eat pig food. I eat balls made of used tea leaves. What I could find. My mother and sisters…I never see again.

The students, they laugh. They don't understand. What life was then. Or under the Japanese. They have so much, they just do not understand.

Jung Guo, China, provide me with evvv-erything I need. I have a roof. A home. My family. When I die, they burn my body for free. Terrible thing, family has old lady die. They can not afford to…but China pay for it. For free.

Yes, during Cultural Revolution, school suffer. Every teacher suffer. But now things are better. Now is Harvest Moon. Tonight we have a feast.

(Everyone toasts: Gam Bei, Kam pai.)

TEACHER CHEN. Here is mud in your eye.

(They all repeat this as well.)

ANDREW. Gam bei.

(He shoots it down. Reacts like he's been electrocuted.)

ANDREW. *(coughing)* What was that?

TEACHER MING. This very special treat. Rice wine and snake bile. Very good for you.

ANDREW. *(coughing)* It's very good.

*(Everyone laughs at **ANDREW**, **YING** in particular. **PAULA** takes his picture.)*

VOICE (VICE PRINCIPAL HUANG). Am I interrupting?

*(All look up, too late, to see, **VICE PRINCIPAL HUANG**. It is as if a snake has entered the room. No one wants to upset him, but no one wants him to stay.)*

TEACHER MING. Vice Principal Huang –

VICE PRINCIPAL HUANG. I heard the party all the way from the bachelor faculty dorm.

TEACHER MING. I hope we are not disturbing your work.

VICE PRINCIPAL HUANG. And I remember, it is Harvest Moon Night. Yes.

TEACHER CHEN. Teacher Bai Ke and Wei Tan hear the same thing. They walk by, and so we want to be good hosts and invite them in.

PAULA & ANDREW. That's right, we were just walking by.

VICE PRINCIPAL HUANG. Quite right. And then I thought, a good party always deserve a special favor.

(He pulls out a bottle of champagne. This means nothing to the locals, but **ANDREW** *and* **PAULA** *can not believe what they are seeing.)*

ANDREW. Is that...

PAULA. Champagne?

VICE PRINCIPAL HUANG. It comes all the way from France, with the compliments of your Mr. Kan. I was waiting for the refrigerator to become sanctioned for operation, but –

TEACHER MING. Doesn't matter. Doesn't matter.

*(***TEACHER MING*** pops the cork and scares the daylights out of* **YING** *in particular. The women pour glasses.)*

TEACHER MING. Gam bei.

VICE PRINCIPAL HUANG. Gam bei.

(Everyone toasts, and drinks. No one is used to drinking, especially with foreigners, especially in front of **VICE PRINCIPAL HUANG.** *They get giddy.)*

TEACHER CHEN. It is quite a good wine, I venture.

XIAO WAN. *(staring at her glass)* Look at all the little bubbles.

*(***YING*** waits to see everyone else has survived drinking it, then gulps his in one.)*

YING. *(gasps, then smiles broadly)* Ho ah. Ho ah.

(The music changes, to the Blue Danube Waltz.)

TEACHER CHEN. This is, I think, a beautiful waltz. Do you agree, Teacher Wei Tan?

PAULA. Yes.

XIAO WAN. What is waltz?

*(***TEACHER CHEN*** stands, and starts to count the rhythm for* **XIAO WAN** *...)*

TEACHER CHEN. *Yi*-er-san. *Yi*-er-san. It has been so long.

PAULA. May I?

*(***TEACHER CHEN*** looks to* **HUANG,** *to make sure it's allowed. He nods.* **TEACHERS CHEN** *and* **WEI TAN** *start to dance. Everyone watches them.)*

TEACHER MING. *(to* ANDREW*)* No one has danced here for many years. You see. Many years.

*(*VICE PRINCIPAL HUANG *goes to* TEACHER MING, *and offers his hand.)*

VICE PRINCIPAL HUANG. May I have the honor, Comrade?

*(*TEACHER MING *looks to* YING, *to see if he'd rather dance.)*

TEACHER MING. Ying, tio' nmah? *(Do you want to dance?)*

WORKER YING. M'tio. M'tio.

*(*YING *smiles, shakes his head. He is happy with his champagne.)*

TEACHER MING. It is my pleasure.

(The old survivor and the new survivor dance as well. PAULA *signals* ANDREW *to dance with* XIAO WAN.*)*

ANDREW. Will you dance with me, Xiao Wan?

(He is awkward. She shyly accepts his offer. ANDREW *now talks and waltzes with* XIAO WAN *while* PAULA *talks and waltzes with* TEACHER CHEN.*)*

PAULA. *(to* TEACHER CHEN*)* You are a very good dancer.

ANDREW. *(to* XIAO WAN*)* I'm not really a good dancer.

TEACHER CHEN. I think I am all toes and have two left feet, may I say this?

XIAO WAN. Nonsense. You are very good on your feet.

PAULA. You may say it, but it is not true. You have very good rhythm, Teacher Chen.

ANDREW. Miss Wei Tan thinks I'm terrible.

TEACHER CHEN. I study music for many years.

PAULA. What do you play?

(Realizes too late this is a bad question.)

TEACHER CHEN. Not now. This is…before. My violin was… destroyed. And my wrists broken. So…now I listen.

PAULA. I'm sorry.

TEACHER CHEN. No bother.

XIAO WAN. *(re: Paula)* She is very beautiful.

ANDREW. Very.

XIAO WAN. I think I am dizzy.

ANDREW. I'll hold you.

(He does.)

TEACHER CHEN. Now everything is better. You see. We dance like when we were young. Thank you Teacher Wei-tan.

XIAO WAN. My father tell me I should tell you I make a good wife for you.

ANDREW. What?

XIAO WAN. I take care of you. And you can be my prince who will come and take me away from Jung Guo. Take me with you to Mei Guo.

ANDREW. I don't think it would be that easy.

XIAO WAN. My daddy also say to tell you Chinese women don't care what their husband looks like, as long as he has lots of money.

ANDREW. Thank you, Xiao Wan.

XIAO WAN. Please Mr. Bai Ke. I can not stay here. No work. No school. Take me with you.

*(She starts to cling to **ANDREW**. He tries to pull back, but she is pleading now.)*

ANDREW. Xiao Wan, let's just sit down.

XIAO WAN. Please Mr. Bai Ke. Please.

*(**HUANG**, others turn to see what is going on. **XIAO WAN**, perhaps a little drunk, is oblivious. **TEACHER CHEN** rushes over to get her to be quiet.)*

*(From cross-stage **WAN** is furious, **HUANG** and **WANG** bow their heads.)*

WIDOW WAN. *(in Cantonese)* Ah Wong, lay duei kuei dei chuen mo hung jai. Yiga gau dou luen tsut bat jou.

(Wang, you have lost control. Do you see what happens.)

PRINCIPAL WANG. Xiao Wan will learn her lesson. It will not happen again.

(She dismisses him with a nod. He nervously leaves. **HUANG** *on trial now.)*

WIDOW WAN. *(in bad Mandarin)* Ni zuo shenma?…Ni shr Shang-hai ren, ma?

VICE PRINCIPAL HUANG. Duei, wo shr Shang-hai ren.

WIDOW WAN. *(Mandarin)* Ni yao jian nide Shanghai laopo, ni zhou kwai ba shiqing gao hao. Yige yue.

(If you want to see your wife [old lady] in Shanghai, you better turns things around. I give you one month.)

(She leaves. He nods.)

(A chill has descended on campus. Dressed in many layers, **PAULA** *fiddles with the lenses of her camera.* **ANDREW** *types feverishly. VOA plays. They seem estranged.)*

VOA ANNOUNCER. You are listening to the Voice of America. The time is now 4AM, Greenwich Mean Time. Once again, our top story, the American hostages in Iran will today mark their second Thanksgiving in captivity amidst reports that they are no longer being held at the Embassy compound…

(The entourage – **WANG**, **HUANG**, **CHEN** *and* **WAN** *across from* **PAULA** *and* **ANDREW**.*)*

PRINCIPAL WANG, CHEN, HUANG, WAN. How are you, Mr. Bai Ke?

PAULA. We're fine.

ANDREW. *(patting his stomach)* Chr bao le.

WIDOW WAN. Chr bao le? Ta shuo chr bao le?

(I have eaten. He said, I have eaten?!)

PRINCIPAL WANG. Widow Wan thinks your Chinese is better than Miss Wei Tan. Yes.

*(**PAULA** shoots **ANDREW** a look.)*

ANDREW. Tea?

TEACHER CHEN. It is not necessary.

> *(They all say no to the tea: "Bu, bu" "Bukeci. Bukeci."* **ANDREW** *ignores this and pours.)*

VICE PRINCIPAL HUANG. No, we can not stay long. We hope we are not disturbing your work.

> *(***WIDOW WAN** *clears her throat, to prompt* **WANG.***)*

PRINCIPAL WANG. Widow Wan wants to know if you enjoy your stay here at the Da Lang Institute?

PAULA. Oh yes. We've been well taken care of. Right Andrew?

ANDREW. Oh yes. Although, to be honest, we have had some –

VICE PRINCIPAL HUANG. *(taking over the deal)* Since you are happy here, then we bring good news. Widow Wan has spoken to the Chief Administrator for Guangdong Foreign Trade Education and he has granted permission for you two to extend your contract.

ANDREW. You're kidding.

VICE PRINCIPAL HUANG. It is nearly the end of the semester, and the students have been quite successful in their studies.

PAULA. Really?

TEACHER CHEN. Yes, and the administration *(indicates* **WIDOW WAN***)* is also quite pleased with your presence here.

ANDREW & PAULA. Huh.

WIDOW WAN. Fai dee. Fai dee ah. *(Go on. Do it.)*

> *(They are obliged to switch tracks, even though it breaks their pitch.)*

PRINCIPAL WANG. Should you decide to not stay, the Da Lang Institute would offer to purchase the bicycles you have used for 300 kwai Chinese ren men bi.

ANDREW. The bicycles. *These* bicycles?

WIDOW WAN. *(nodding)* Duei. *(correct)*

VICE PRINCIPAL HUANG. It is more convenient that they stay here. And the typewriter. Since you neglected to declare them upon arrival, it is unlikely you will be allowed to remove them. But we, may I say, would rather you stay here with them.

ANDREW. You know, speaking of the bikes –

PAULA. Andrew –

ANDREW. – I wouldn't have had to buy them, if –

(Sensing trouble, **VICE PRINCIPAL HUANG** *covers quickly, to avoid arousing* **WIDOW WAN***'s concern.)*

VICE PRINCIPAL HUANG. Of course, our proposition is most fair, but if you need time to think it over…

PAULA. Yes, I think that is right. Time –

ANDREW. – to think it over.

PRINCIPAL WANG. We will await your acceptance of our fair offer. The Department of Foreign Trade Education would like to know at your earliest convenience, but in any event no later than the first of the month.

WIDOW WAN. Gole. Xie xie. Xie xie.

*(***WIDOW WAN** *starts to stand. Everyone immediately follows her move.)*

PAULA & ANDREW/WANG ET AL. Zai jian.

TEACHER CHEN. *(to* **PAULA***, at door)* Happy Thanksgiving.

PAULA. Thank you.

(The entourage leaves.)

PAULA. They want us to *stay?*

ANDREW. They can't be serious.

(Outside their door, **WAN** *turns to* **HUANG***.)*

WIDOW WAN. *(in Cantonese inflected Mandarin)* Shanghai ren, ni bu xiang diu mian, ni zhou ba ta-men liu xia lai.

(Shanghai ren: If you want to save face, you better hope they stay.)

VICE PRINCIPAL HUANG. Than you, Widow Wan.

(She leaves, with **WANG** *in tow.* **HUANG** *turns to* **CHEN**.)*

VICE PRINCIPAL HUANG. Teacher Chen, you do think they will renew?

TEACHER CHEN. They did say they've been well taken care of.

VICE PRINCIPAL HUANG. You have a Special Relationship, with Miss Wheaton. I would be very grateful, for any help you can give.

TEACHER CHEN. I will do my utmost.

(Cross stage, **SHERMAN**, *playing with dice, lies in wait for* **ANDREW**.)*

SHERMAN. Mr. Bai Ke!

ANDREW. Sherman.

SHERMAN. There is much news on the narrow pathways today. The first rumor is, last month's Harvest Moon Party has resulted in many self-criticisms. Vice Principal Huang and Principal Wang are hanging on by a thread.

ANDREW. Because we went to a party.

SHERMAN. Not just the party. The scandal is further caused by the shameful actions of Xiao Wan.

(laughing)

Did she really propose to you?

ANDREW. She was…oh god, they're not going to do anything to her.

SHERMAN. Everyone thinks she will be sent very far away, to reform school or labor camp.

ANDREW. She was just –

SHERMAN. But she may yet dodge the bullet. Because of the other rumor.

ANDREW. What? Don't play with me Sherman, what?

SHERMAN. This one you already know. Your teaching contract is almost up. And Widow Wan has offered you and Miss Wei Tan a generous and fair offer to extend.

ANDREW. What does that have to do with –

SHERMAN. The school still can not get permission for official Foreign Experts, and so, they have decided to continue to make lemon out of lemonade, may I say this.

ANDREW. Close enough –

SHERMAN. The rumor further says your salary will be raised.

ANDREW. It's not really negotiable. I have to get home –

SHERMAN. Everything is negotiable in Guangdong. Even Xiao Wan. The school is afraid if they send her away, neither one of you will stay. So, for now, her fate is in your hands.

ANDREW. But Paula and I, we have to go.

SHERMAN. And she is waving at you.

ANDREW. What?

PAULA. *(running on)* Andrew!

SHERMAN. You now are the one who is in a quandary. If you tell her, she will not want to go. If she stay, what will you do. They have you now, like the rest of us.

PAULA. Andrew!

ANDREW. What!

PAULA. Come quick.

ANDREW. I'm in the middle of a game.

PAULA. Andrew!

ANDREW. Can't it goddamn –

(He looks at her, sees it's serious. He goes over.)

What? What –

PAULA. Listen.

(She holds up their radio.)

VOA ANNOUNCER. Repeating. In New York City tonight, former Beatle John Lennon was shot and killed by a gunman outside his apartment building on Manhattan's Upper West Side.

(They look at each other. Shaken, they walk back to their room as the students watch, and try to make sense of what has happened.)

VOA ANNOUNCER. *(on exit, as needed)* According to witnesses at the scene, the gunman called out the singer's name, then shot him at point blank range. A suspect is reportedly being held by New York City police. Within minutes of the shooting, thousands of mourners gathered for a candlelight vigil outside the Dakota apartment building where Lennon lived with wife Yoko Ono. Similar vigils have now gathered in cities throughout the world to play Lennon's music.

(Time shift. **ANDREW** *and* **PAULA** *alone in the apartment. Moving boxes are packed, shelves bare.)*

ANDREW. They haven't heard of Greek civilization, ok fine. Freud, the Renaissance, the Marx *Brothers*. Fine. There's not one phone for the entire campus; they think Edelweiss is our National Anthem – That's fine. I can deal with it. But the Beatles. How is that possible?

PAULA. Why should our students know the Beatles?

ANDREW. I don't know…I mean, your right: that's why we're here. The school just wants us to be accent and phrasing machines, but the students, they want us to teach them "everything that's happened outside of China since time began."

PAULA. Lucky for them, you know it all. Everyone likes you, you've made friends.

ANDREW. *Friends?* You can't have any friends here – everyone's either spying, or on the make. Xiao Wan wants me to get her out of the country. Sherman wants me to smuggle.

PAULA. And whose fault is that?

ANDREW. What –

PAULA. I warned you about flirting with Xiao Wan. And the bikes, Andrew. You showed him you were corruptible.

ANDREW. I didn't flirt with – You and your Western guilt – do you get what goes on here? They're going to blackmail us. If we leave, Xiao Wan gets sent away.

PAULA. Andrew, they wouldn't do that –

ANDREW. You have no idea how this place works. Your fuck-ing family told you the Cultural Revolution was a great social experiment, so you can't see this place for what it really is –

PAULA. And you can? C'mon Andrew, we're all blind here. They don't know anything about us, we don't know anything about them. You're no different from them. You think New York is the center of the world, they think Guangzhou is. They're both just two push pins on the globe, Andrew. I don't understand why you came here. I really don't.

(She walks out.)

ANDREW. *(to himself)* I came here to be with you.

*(**PAULA** re-enters, for her cigarettes.)*

PAULA. Did you say something?

*(He picks up a few boxes, and walks out. **PAULA**, alone, lights a cigarette. After a beat, there's a knock on the door.)*

VICE PRINCIPAL HUANG. Teacher Wei Tan? Hello.

*(**PAULA** takes one last puff on her cigarette. Puts it out. Goes to door.)*

PAULA. Vice Principal Huang. Andrew just left...to the post office. He'll be back in –

VICE PRINCIPAL HUANG. Actually, I was wondering if I might have a word with you.

PAULA. Me?

(He enters the living room. Looks at the boxes.)

VICE PRINCIPAL HUANG. If this is not a good time, of course –

PAULA. No come in. Please. Excuse the...we're getting ready to...

VICE PRINCIPAL HUANG. So I see.

PAULA. It was a difficult decision to –

VICE PRINCIPAL HUANG. I am sorry to hear of your loss, Teacher Wei Tan. The students tell of how sad you are about…Mr. Le-Nin, is it?

PAULA. Len-*non*. Different spelling, "o-n," not…Listen to me. I can't stop teaching. I'm sorry.

VICE PRINCIPAL HUANG. Not at all. The students say he was a singer of peace.

PAULA. Yes. We didn't know what to do. No one here knows him. And, well, I hope you don't mind, we taught a class about him today.

VICE PRINCIPAL HUANG. I know.

PAULA. Yes. Of course you do.

VICE PRINCIPAL HUANG. There are not many secrets in Da Lang, Teacher Wei Tan.

PAULA. Sometimes, I've felt like it's all secrets….Tea?

VICE PRINCIPAL HUANG. Bu ke ci. Bu bu bu.

(She pours. He offers her a cigarette.)

VICE PRINCIPAL HUANG. Cigarette?

(She starts to say no.)

That's right, the students tell me you are…"trying to cut back." Is this correct.

PAULA. *(taking the cigarette)* Grammatically, if not in truth.

VICE PRINCIPAL HUANG. Just so. Teacher Wei Tan.

(He lights hers, then his own.)

PAULA. Would it kill you to…call me Paula.

VICE PRINCIPAL HUANG. I can try…Bao Le. This means, a flower ready to bloom. Bao Le.

(They are immediately far more intimate.)

VICE PRINCIPAL HUANG. *(cont.)* I come also to let you know the school is most sorry to learn of your decision to not renew your contracts.

PAULA. So are we.

VICE PRINCIPAL HUANG. China, I think, has been a difficult experience for you. You are used to so much more. I have spoken to the Guangdong Ministry of Education, about your salary –

PAULA. It's not about the money –

VICE PRINCIPAL HUANG. Yes of course. The students joke that you and Teacher Bai Ke are the only ones in Guangdong who still want to bicycle on the Socialist Road.

PAULA. Andrew has to go back. He has many family pressures.

VICE PRINCIPAL HUANG. And I think, also, if he stays much longer, he will have no meat on his bones left at all.

PAULA. So you see –

VICE PRINCIPAL HUANG. I just wanted to make sure you were aware the school would be happy to have either one of you stay. It is not, may I say, a package deal.

PAULA. Pardon?

VICE PRINCIPAL HUANG. You are a very good teacher.

PAULA. No, I'm not. I wish I could be. I'm a just a beginner. We know you were hoping for teachers with more experience.

VICE PRINCIPAL HUANG. At first, yes. But you have turned out to be very good, Very good. All the students and teachers say so.

PAULA. Mr. Bai Ke is the one who really keeps the classes moving.

VICE PRINCIPAL HUANG. He is also good, and a "quick study." But he, if I may say, sees things here in terms of good or bad. White and black. Yes?…

(**PAULA** *does not answer this.*)

You see our school in terms of what you can give, and what you can learn. Is that not so?

(**PAULA** *again does not answer.*)

VICE PRINCIPAL HUANG. *(cont.)* We do not have much to offer you, I know. But you are needed here. It takes time for the administration to adjust to having foreigners. You have come to understand us, and we to understand you. With time, there is more trust, you see.

PAULA. Trust has been hard to come by.

VICE PRINCIPAL HUANG. The administration has made mistakes –

PAULA. Aren't you the administration?

VICE PRINCIPAL HUANG. I am a cadre, I must represent many departments. Enforce many policies. Get much information.

PAULA. Even at Harvest Moon Ball?

VICE PRINCIPAL HUANG. I am trying to protect her. I promise you...

(off her reaction)

It is very difficult to know that there is a better way, but to have to do one's job...

(He begins to drop his guard.)

Always so in China. Too many favors throughout the system. You want medicine. Good meat? A ride to the hospital for your ailing grandmother so you don't have to put her on the back of your bicycle for ten miles? Well, what can you do for me?

(can not help himself anymore)

You want to live with your wife in Shanghai, instead of living 800 miles away in Canton where everyone despise you – what can you do for me? What can you tell me about what so and so thinks? He said *what* about the Cultural Revolution? He said Mao was a great leader, but he *didn't* say "the revolution started well and then mistakes were made?" Thank you. You may go. I'll let you know about your transfer.

Curry favor. Always. Curry favor by betraying friends. I think at most, in China, everyone can have one or two friend. At most. Even those, you might not trust when times are rough.

I wish we could say what we think, without having to say something else two weeks later. I wish we could work where we want to. I wish the government would leave us alone…I wish –

I'm sorry. I am talking nonsense. It is –

PAULA. No. Please. It's alright.

VICE PRINCIPAL HUANG. I don't know. Sometimes, I think, you are the only ones here anyone can trust, because you are always free to go. As you are about to do.

PAULA. Mr. Bai Ke is really not – he has to get out.

VICE PRINCIPAL HUANG. Yes, I know. He has his mind made up. But your mind is open, Miss Wei Tan. Bao Le. And if you were on your own, I think you would find it much easier to get to know us. One on one. You will think it over. Please.

(He leaves. She stands, overwhelmed. Exits as a more than 20 year time shift takes place.)

(Sound of a plane landing.)

(Cross stage now, a Chinese Customs man, looks up from his computer.)

CUSTOMS MAN. Next.

*(**ANDREW BAKER** approaches warily.)*

ANDREW. Foreigners of Non-Chinese extraction?

(It is 20 odd years later. His bags are better. He wears a sports coat. He hands his papers over.)

CUSTOMS MAN. Welcome back, Mr. Baker.

ANDREW. Pardon.

CUSTOMS MAN. This is not your first visit to China.

ANDREW. It's been a long time.

CUSTOMS MAN. You were here, right after the…lost decade.

(ANDREW nods.)

CUSTOMS MAN. Everything has changed Mr. Baker. China is now, very modern, very up to date. We have skyscrapers, and cell phones. And traffic jams.

ANDREW. I should feel right at home.

CUSTOMS MAN. We welcome you back and wish you good luck on your journey. Do you have plans for these days?

ANDREW. I'll stay in town. Maybe rent a bike, and go to the Monument to the 72 Martyrs of the Guangzhou Uprising.

CUSTOMS MAN. The what?

ANDREW. My old haunt.

CUSTOMS MAN. Yes, of course.

(He hands him his passport. ANDREW walks across stage. To Da Lang.)

(PAULA pours him tea. End of the day.)

PAULA. So, how was the journey?

(remembering)

Pleasant, I hope. Not too cold, not too warm.

ANDREW. Very pleasant, indeed.

(They share the memory.)

…they're not still using those are they.

PAULA. No. It's too bad, I liked having the students sound like you.

ANDREW. And yet, you never wrote.

(a few awkward beats)

PAULA. More tea?

(He nods, she pours.)

Start over?…How's your writing.

ANDREW. My what – Oh god, it has been a long time. Um… let's see…I came home – without you – Sorry. I had my diaries. And I tried to sell a novel. My "agent" looked at it, said, "China don't sell, kid." That was that. He got me some ghosting work. Which led to corporate speeches…and I don't know how it happened but I've become, forgive me, a businessman.

PAULA. Andrew, I'm not judging.

ANDREW. No, I am. I mean look at you: the keeper of the flame.

PAULA. There's no flame here. I don't know if there ever was, you know that.

ANDREW. But all these years –

PAULA. At first it was going to be one month. To train the new teachers. But they had difficulties getting visas. So I finished the semester. And then…I started to do some counseling. My brother sent me books on Post-traumatic stress.

ANDREW. Barefoot shrink?

PAULA. I called it Advanced Grammar, more convenient.

ANDREW. I don't know how you – I didn't realize it then, but…it wasn't the bureaucracy that drove me crazy. I just couldn't handle how much pain everyone was in.

PAULA. I'd never have made it through the first months without you.

ANDREW. But you…you've been fine? This whole time?

PAULA. Very…Every few years a cold wind blows from the north. But I never get in trouble, just sometimes the people who talk to me. I'm…I'm a Special Friend of China now. That's a very high ranking. Did you know, even at the height of the Cultural Revolution, no one touched the Special Friends of China? Dozens of fangweilos in Beijing lived through the whole thing, their privileges intact. 'Til the day they died.

(He reacts to "died," then covers it up.)

ANDREW. Privileges? You wouldn't let them do our laundry.

PAULA. I don't know what I was thinking. Today, Teacher Wei Tan has her own machine. State of the art. Three socks at a time.

ANDREW. Do you see them. The Da Lang class of 81?

PAULA. Sometimes. The "post Cultural Revolution genera-
tion" – they're running the factories, the corporations
– and they are not looking back.

ANDREW. The company I work for…they're outsourcing.
I'm going to be their Compliance Officer – it's my job
to make sure the local managers don't turn the factories into sweat shops.

PAULA. Good luck with that.

ANDREW. So the school was right to worry about us – we
really did pave the way for the Capitalist road. Talk
about the law of unintended consequences.

PAULA. I'm not sure how unintended it was. They knew.
The door had to open. So they let a few believers in, to
build up resistance.

ANDREW. And now the sleeping giant has awakened. It's in
all the papers.

PAULA. Oh, the giant woke up a long time ago. Americans
just never notice, til the giant gets hungry. Do people
in the states even realize their empire is ending?

ANDREW. Not so much. Letting go has never been one of
our strong suits.

(looks at her)

God Paula, you look great.

PAULA. Andrew, I'm sorry.

ANDREW. What?

PAULA. For the way we…the way I handled…

ANDREW. It's ok. We were kids, we didn't know how to –

PAULA. No. It's not ok. I should have told you I was staying.
Instead of letting you find out, on the day of…

ANDREW. What difference does it make. Now.

PAULA. No it matters. To be understood. To know what
happened. Even now. So I'm sorry.

ANDREW. We both are. I mean, let's face it, I was a jerk.

PAULA. You were. And I was a coward. I was afraid, if I told you I was staying, you'd have talked me out of it. I needed to stay, to prove to myself I could do it on my own.

ANDREW. Sherman used to tease me. Wo ai ni, ni ai Jun guo. Jung guo ai qian.

PAULA. You love me, I love China, China loves money.

ANDREW. He was right, at least about me. You were the only reason I went in the first place.

PAULA. Now you are talking nonsense, Andrew Baker.

ANDREW. No.

(sips his tea)

So, um…what happened to Vice Principal Huang. He was the one who convinced you to stay, wasn't he.

PAULA. He was. And he was…reassigned to his home in Shanghai, a little after you left. His pay-off, I guess, for getting me to stay.

ANDREW. There's a shock. Did he blackmail you, about Xiao Wan.

PAULA. No, Andrew. He wasn't like that.

ANDREW. Really.

PAULA. Really. All he did was…he talked. To me. He was, you won't believe this, very sincere. Underneath. In another world, he would have been a poet, or…a compliance officer. Here he did what he had to do, like everybody else. He was an honorable man.

ANDREW. It all worked out, I guess.

PAULA. We just talked, and, the next thing I knew, I looked up and –

ANDREW. You could still come home. Everyone in the states has a mid-life crisis. It's encouraged.

PAULA. No. It's not my home anymore…This is.

ANDREW. Paula.

PAULA. Remember what Lincoln told us, when we first came here?

ANDREW. You'd be amazed at what I don't remember.

PAULA. You don't have to be…glib all the time.

ANDREW. I know. He said, "Inside outside have difference."

PAULA. Wherever…we end up, we spend our time misinterpreting, leaving things unsaid. And I sometimes think this became my life because, for one hour, on a winter's afternoon, inside outside had no difference.

The End

OTHER TITLES AVAILABLE FROM SAMUEL FRENCH

MAYOR

Music and Lyrics by Charles Strouse
Book by Warren Leight
Based on the book *Mayor* by Edward I. Koch

Musical Revue / 4m, 4f / Bare Stage

If you love New York – or if you hate it – you will be sure to enjoy this peppy show, which is as much about life in the Big Apple as it is about the Mayor. Virtually every aspect of the social and political life of New York City is genially lampooned, and the result is an entertaining evening – even for audiences who wouldn't be able to tell Ed Koch from Frank Perdue!

"An extremely entertaining blend of polemic, satire,
song and dance."
– *Women's Wear Daily*

"While Mayor Koch has been called many things by his fans and detractors, adjectives like "genial, mild' and "sweet' have generally not been among them. It's those words, however, that most accurately describe both Mayor and the character it places center stage."
– *The New York Times*

OTHER TITLES AVAILABLE FROM SAMUEL FRENCH

CHING CHONG CHINAMAN

Lauren Yee

Comedy / 3m, 3f

The Wongs are American as apple pie. Desdemona dreams of Princeton but could use some help with her calculus. Her brother Upton wants to be a World of Warcraft champion but needs more free time to train. Upton solves both their problems by bringing an indentured servant home one day, but they soon discover that "Ching Chong" has American dreams of his own!

An irreverent new comedy by Lauren Yee is skewering every cliché about Asian American identity. The show won the 2007 Yale Playwrights Festival.

"A lively, likable show! Playwright Lauren Yee gleefully highlights the assimilated life of the Wongs, who defy the stereotype of the hard driving Chinese-American family. It's clever and her insights are astute!"
— *The New York Times*

"A wildly inventive, raucously funny ride. Though rooted in Asian American literary tradition, this play upends its conventions with inspired irreverence. You have not seen anything like this before. The fourth wave of Asian American playwriting has arrived!"
— David Henry Hwang, *The New York Times*

"A smart, fast-paced comedy that wrings laughs from the topics of cultural identity and assimilation. Neither predictable nor politically correct, it's a satirical cartoon that has heart and even occasional poignancy"
— *TheatreMania.com*

OTHER TITLES AVAILABLE FROM SAMUEL FRENCH

YEAR ZERO

Michael Golamco

Dramatic Comedy / 3m, 1f

Vuthy Vichea is sixteen years old, Cambodian American. He loves hip hop and Dungeons and Dragons. He has thick-ass glasses. He is a weird kid in a place where weirdness can be fatal: Long Beach, California. Since his best friend moved and his mother died, the only person he can talk to is a human skull he keeps hidden in a cookie jar. *Year Zero* is a comedic drama about young Cambodian Americans — about reincarnation, reinvention, and ultimately, redemption.

"[A] tenderly observed play… These characters are cut from familiar molds, but Mr. Golamco and his appealing cast bring fresh nuances, tempering the earnestness with unassuming charm."
– The New York Times

"A very smart, sweet, honest and uncommonly moving new play… Michael Golamco is a significant new dramatic voice."
– The Chicago Tribune

"A delicate portrait of lost souls attempting to discover their roots and navigate awkward relationships with one another… Incisive, both dramatically and thematically, leading to a haunting and hopeful climax. Critic's Pick!"
– Backstage

www.ingramcontent.com/pod-product-compliance
Lightning Source LLC
Chambersburg PA
CBHW070642120726
47909CB00004B/1540